Once upon a time live
fund-raising consultan

She arranged programs for schoolteachers who wanted to raise
money for student projects. Lo, a mean, grizzly man taught in a
dark, foreboding classroom at Western High, and he was the one she
feared the most. Every day he would pace back and forth before his
chalkboard, wondering how he would tongue-lash the poor fund-
raising consultant the next time she called. And every day she
would brave the phone lines to carry on a decent conversation with
him. She tried to help him organize a program that would raise the
money he needed. But, alas, she didn't know if triumph or failure
existed in her future.

Lindsay Thomas snapped open her eyes and giggled. *What a
fairy tale that would make. The mean teacher versus the innocent
fund-raising consultant. The only question was, Would it have a
happy ending?*

LAURALEE BLISS is a multi-published author of award-winning inspirational fiction. Lauralee enjoys writing novels that are reminiscent of a roller coaster ride for the reader. Her desire is that readers will turn the pages until they reach the end and come away with both an entertaining story and a lesson that ministers to the heart. Besides writing, Lauralee home schools her son and enjoys gardening, roaming yard sales, visiting historical sites, and hiking a mountain trail. She invites you to visit her web site at: www.lauraleebliss.com

Books by Lauralee Bliss

HEARTSONG PRESENTS
HP249—Mountaintop
HP333—Behind the Mask
HP457—A Rose Among Thorns

Don't miss out on any of our super romances. Write to us at the following address for information on our newest releases and club information.

Heartsong Presents Readers' Service
PO Box 719
Uhrichsville, OH 44683

Or visit www.heartsongpresents.com

A Storybook Finish

Lauralee Bliss

Heartsong Presents

To the fund-raising reps and workers of Great American and their families, many of whom are ardent readers and supporters of my books. Thank you so much!

With thanks to Stephen McDowell and the Providence Foundation for the use of their book, "In God We Trust Tour Guide" in the writing of this novel.

A note from the author:
I love to hear from my readers! You may correspond with me by writing:

Lauralee Bliss
Author Relations
PO Box 719
Uhrichsville, OH 44683

ISBN 1-58660-834-7

A STORYBOOK FINISH

Copyright © 2003 by Lauralee Bliss. All rights reserved. Except for use in any review, the reproduction or utilization of this work in whole or in part in any form by any electronic, mechanical, or other means, now known or hereafter invented, is forbidden without the permission of Heartsong Presents, an imprint of Barbour Publishing, Inc., PO Box 719, Uhrichsville, Ohio 44683.

All Scripture quotations are taken from the King James Version of the Bible.

All of the characters and events in this book are fictitious. Any resemblance to actual persons, living or dead, or to actual events is purely coincidental.

PRINTED IN THE U.S.A.

one

Once upon a time lived a crazy, stressed-out, fund-raising consultant. She arranged programs for schoolteachers who wanted to raise money for student projects. Lo, a mean, grizzly man taught in a dark, foreboding classroom at Western High, and he was the one she feared the most. Every day he would pace back and forth before his chalkboard, wondering how he would tongue-lash the poor fund-raising consultant the next time she called. And every day she would brave the phone lines to carry on a decent conversation with him. She tried to help him organize a program that would raise the money he needed. But, alas, she didn't know if triumph or failure existed in her future.

Lindsay Thomas snapped open her eyes and giggled. *What a fairy tale that would make. The mean teacher versus the innocent fund-raising consultant. The only question was, Would it have a happy ending?* She shook her head. *Enough of that. I have work to do.*

She pulled out a checklist and scanned it. "Sponsor folders, prize poster fliers, classroom envelopes, team goal charts. Uh, prize bag full of toys, prospect lists—" She halted and whirled to the empty cabinet. "My brochures for the sale! If my brochures aren't delivered today, I can't kick off that fundraiser in the morning at Western High. That history teacher will have my head on a silver platter."

Wading through the cardboard boxes in her office that contained previous shipments, Lindsay managed to reach the front door of her apartment. On the stone steps sat three mangled boxes bound with tape, dropped off by the delivery-man. No doubt they had been tossed in the back of some dirty truck like garbage. The ripped corners of the boxes revealed the slick, colored paper poking out of their shrink-wrap. The corners were crinkled from the rough treatment.

With a groan, Lindsay dragged in the first box that must have weighed forty pounds. She inhaled a breath to calm her rapid heartbeat and lugged in the other boxes. She then plopped down on the carpet to complete the destruction the delivery service had apparently started.

At least they're here. She sighed. The brochures showed pic-tures of chocolates and other treats the students would sell to family and friends. Now she had everything to kick off the fund-raising event bright and early the next morning.

When the history teacher, Jeff Wheeler, had called on the phone a few weeks back, asking her for a painless promotion so the junior class could raise money for the prom, Lindsay was delighted. She loved the idea of doing a program at her alma mater, Western High. She talked him into signing up for a program in which the students would sell items from a brochure and which guaranteed the money he requested.

Instead of the usual enthusiasm she received from teachers eager for revenue to meet their needs, Jeff Wheeler had grumbled. "Why I was appointed to do this is beyond me," he said gruffly. "I've been in this school only a year, and they lay this responsibility on me. They must like the idea of initiating fresh blood. 'Here's the peon of the teaching force. Let him run the fund-raiser for the junior class.'"

"I'm sorry to hear that, but—"

"I was hired to teach history, the same as you're hired to

conduct fund-raisers. I never spotted the junior prom on my list of teaching responsibilities. It's just another thing I have to do. My plate is full enough as it is."

Lindsay wondered if the guy was really this uptight or if life in general treated him badly. Maybe his wife had burnt the morning toast or shrunk his favorite Rugby shirt in the wash. He rattled on about the quizzes he still had to correct while Lindsay thought back to her own junior prom and the wonderful time she'd had with a guy named Ron. She had pleasant memories of the evening—great dancing, good food, and a lovely corsage with a scent that carried her across the dance floor. She'd never spent more on a dress in her life. Unfortunately, after graduation, Ron left for college on the West Coast. They hadn't spoken in years.

Jeff Wheeler continued. "These students need history more than a prom, if you ask me. No one can tell you anything about the history of our nation. When I ask the classes what ship the Pilgrims sailed on, they say the Carnival Cruise Line."

"I'm sure they're just joking," Lindsay managed to say when Jeff paused to draw a breath. She never knew guys to be talkative, but this one had already outdone himself in ten minutes. Maybe he had to get things off his chest.

"One student actually put that answer on a test. I took ten points off his paper. His father called me up, asking me why I took off ten points when the question was worth only three. When I told him I wouldn't tolerate that kind of answer on a test, the father said I had no sense of humor. He said I should give the kid twenty points for creativity. Sure I would, if this were a creative writing class. This is history. They're supposed to know historical facts. I wish the parents would also understand that."

Lindsay looked at her watch, thinking about the other clients still awaiting her attention that day. She wondered how long he would ramble on. This was a primary fault of hers, the inability to cut off clients when they were in the midst of a diatribe. She felt that if she did interrupt she would face a cancelled contract. That would mean less in sales and less money in her pocket.

"And I might as well tell you," he went on, "I'm not thrilled about working with salespeople. I've had bad experiences with telemarketers. And those vacuum cleaning people who knock on your door in the middle of dinner, forcing you to eat a plate of cold spaghetti—"

Lindsay dearly wanted to interrupt and move on to other things. She prayed the sales figures for this group would outweigh the time lost in contacting other clients.

Jeff continued. "The kind that want to pick your pocket when your back is turned. I don't trust them. The only reason I'm even doing this project is to try to get my foot in the door of this school. I want to do some great things, like a history club, for example. Or maybe even a history quiz bowl. But all that needs money."

"Sounds like some fine ideas the students would appreciate," Lindsay interjected, surprised she could sneak a word in edgewise. "Perhaps after this project you would consider raising money for those events?"

"This is plenty for me to handle right now. If this fund-raiser is a bust, then it won't happen. How do you plan to ensure its success?"

"We have a wonderful prize program to motivate the students to sell."

"What kind of prizes? Not that cheap stuff you spend five

bucks to win at the county fair."

Lindsay proceeded to tell him about the prizes: animated phones, lava lamps, cameras, CD players. She also told him about the first-day prizes and how the beginning of the sale was critical to its success.

"Well, Miss Thomas, I expect it to be painless and profitable. I haven't the time or the gumption to deal with problems. Fund-raising is a necessary evil, but there's nothing I can do about it. I'm saddled with it. You understand, correct?"

Lindsay offered a salute to the phone sitting on the desk while answering with a calm, "I'll do my best to ensure a satisfactory program, Mr. Wheeler." She knew the importance of instilling confidence in an irate teacher as she had been taught to do in sales school. Yet all she wanted to do was get off the phone and run to the bathroom for an aspirin to relieve her headache.

"Just be sure you raise me the money I need, and everything will be dandy."

This guy's a genuine toad on a lily pad, she thought, returning to her prep work for the fund-raising start. How someone could live with a person like that went beyond her sense of reasoning. During the last few days leading up to the sale, Lindsay contemplated the success of the project. The idea of initiating a program with an agitated sponsor did not bode well for its success. Lindsay, however, was determined to make it work. She had dealt with teachers' emotions in the past. She would put her best foot forward and do what needed to be done to raise Jeff Wheeler the money he required. In the end, he would sing her praises. That was the essence of her job as a fund-raising consultant.

Lindsay carried a stack of brochures to the office, nearly

tripping over a cardboard box left from a shipment of prizes. Prizes, she knew, were the key to motivating the students to sell. If they sold a certain number of items from the brochure, they won the prizes: from banks filled with candy to stuffed cartoon characters, to a radio or even a talking telephone.

She had sat up for hours one night studying the prizes, making mental notes on how she would present the items to generate enthusiasm among the students. In the conferences she attended, the speakers told the sales reps how to make the most out of their presentations. Playing with the prizes in front of the student body was part of the game plan. She went over it all step by step, everything she would need to relate to the students, all the information in the mere twenty minutes Jeff Wheeler had allotted for the assembly. Again, she winced at the tone of his voice that spoke of his control over the situation.

"You get a twenty-minute assembly, and that's all I can give," he'd told her when she discussed aspects of the presentation only yesterday. "I have enough trying to teach my classes with the amount of time they give me on the schedule. Please don't waste time going over details unrelated to the sale. Make it short and simple."

"I feel sorry for his wife," Lindsay grumbled, placing the materials she would need for the next day inside a crate. *The Bible says contentious wives are the ones that live in the corner of a roof. What about contentious men? Do they live in the basement? Actually, he belongs in a pond where he can croak out his problems to his heart's content. I'm not to blame for his predicament with the junior class.* She exhaled loudly. Her breath fluffed the pale brown bangs sweeping across her forehead. *All I do in this job is deal with other people's hang-ups. No wonder I have no energy left to handle my own.*

Her hands began to shake while trying to put a folder of envelopes inside the crate. This pent-up anxiety over Jeff Wheeler and the presentation would never help her in the end. She paused in her work to offer up a prayer for God's favor. Not long ago, she had heard a famous preacher share words of wisdom about one's thought life. No matter what she might construe about Jeff and his personality, she must shift her mind to good thoughts about the upcoming program.

Think on things that are true and of good repute, she recalled from Scripture. *Okay. The students are gonna love the prizes. The Silly Slammers and Goofy phone will talk right on cue so the entire assembly goes wild. In the end, Jeff Wheeler will smile and thank me for a job well done.* Lindsay nodded at this array of thoughts that replaced the doubt.

That evening she doused any remaining flames of worry with music from her favorite CD, along with a relaxing bubble bath. *Everything will go fine,* she reasoned to herself, tracing a path through the bubbles. *Jeff Wheeler will be civil, and the fund-raising program will be a huge success. Oh, Lord, only You can make that happen.*

⋩

Jeff Wheeler rubbed his index fingers across his temples, feeling a sudden headache coming on. It didn't do him a bit of good to get stressed out over a silly fund-raising project, yet he couldn't help it. Having been at this teaching post only a year, he was still trying to get used to the way things were done at Western High. What he didn't plan on was teachers looking down their noses at him. Nothing like this had happened at his last teaching position. At first he thought it was the way he dressed. Or maybe they had all flunked history and he reminded them of their failures.

He recalled a confrontation with a teacher who had stopped by the lounge shortly after he landed the job. Jeff had come there for a cup of coffee and some peace of mind. He poured the coffee and decided the best place to find peace was in the Bible. The teacher stumbled upon him reading his Bible. Her face turned the oddest shade of red. Her eyes bugged out of her head as if he held a pipe bomb in his hands.

"Don't tell me you're going to indoctrinate our students with that thing!"

The "thing" resting on Jeff's lap happened to be a book of power with life-changing capabilities. The teacher threw back her head in a huff when he told her he was merely reading it to find some peace. For Jeff, the Bible meant life. Without that book, he would've likely ended up a drunk somewhere in a dark alley.

Jeff had grown up in a family where success was measured by academics. He loved history and always had his face in a history book, courtesy of his professor-father who kept him well-supplied. The students took to calling him The Worm because he read so much. In college, it was the same. The other students would party away, and he would be in the library. At last, the pressure to conform became too great. He took to drinking beer like everyone else. The drinking made him popular and helped him forget the responsibility and the pressure, or at least he thought it did. He drank frequently after that.

A few months later, several young men invited him to a Christian meeting, and there he found Christ. From that day forward, he studied the Bible, along with his history books, and never touched another beer. God was in control, except when Jeff allowed situations to rob him of his peace, like this junior class fund-raising venture.

Jeff grimaced when he thought of the money going toward the junior prom. It dredged up memories of his high school days. He recalled how he was one out of four guys in the entire class who didn't attend. Not that he didn't try. The girl he asked said yes, then turned around and accepted another invitation behind his back. Jeff had buried his hurt all those years, only to have it rear its ugly head now in a bag full of memories.

He looked down at the leather Bible resting on the coffee table, the binding falling apart and papers jammed in it. If only life could be easy. If only he didn't allow the pressure to get to him. He needed that Bible now, more than ever.

Jeff slid onto the sofa. Before him on the coffee table, amid quizzes to grade and his worn Bible, rested the paperwork for the fund-raising project. He noticed the signature on the contract. Lindsay Thomas. She had nice handwriting and a nice name too, even if she seemed a bit too domineering for his taste. Her control over the project gnawed at him. She had to understand something. This was his show, not hers. His reputation was on the line if things didn't work out. He had made so many plans, too. Failure was not an option. This fund-raiser had to succeed.

Just then the phone rang. He grabbed it up to find the loud voice of Mrs. Coates, the English teacher, barking on the other end. She immediately asked him why he had scheduled a fund-raising assembly during her English class, of all things. When he politely told her he too was losing time from his own class, her voice escalated.

"Well, this can't happen, Jeff. I've scheduled a vocabulary test, and I'm not postponing it. You'll have to move this assembly of yours to another date."

He opened his mouth, ready to tell her he didn't want to do the dumb project in the first place, but teachers like her had stuck his name on it without his consent. If she didn't like how he ran things, she could do it herself. He never said any of those things. Mrs. Coates was a bigwig in the school, having been there longer than anyone. He swallowed a retort and asked, "What day would work out for you?"

Her voice dropped a decibel. "Next Tuesday, I suppose."

"Tuesday. All right. I'll switch it with the fund-raising consultant." The phone clicked in his ear. *So much for relieving pressure. Now I've added more to my life.* He looked up Lindsay's phone number to tell her about the change. It rang endlessly. He tried four different times, without success. "Probably out with her boyfriend, grabbing dinner and a late night movie," he grumbled, tossing the cordless phone on the couch. Why that fact would bother him, he didn't know. Right now, his head and his confidence felt as if they were being crushed between two lead plates. His fingers reached for the Bible. *God, help me get through this.*

two

"I see you like to stay out late."

Lindsay glanced up to find Jeff Wheeler staring at her and the crate of supplies she carried into the auditorium. With thirty minutes remaining before the presentation, Lindsay hoped to set up a good display and still have time to gather her wits. Instead, she found the sponsor glaring down at her with his piercing blue eyes. If he didn't seem so fierce at that moment, she might have gazed at his eyes more intently, thinking how they reminded her of a clear March sky. "Excuse me?"

"I tried calling you at least four times last night. I didn't even get an answering machine. Not a very good business practice."

Confusion assailed her. *Did the phone ring? I never heard it ring, and I was home all evening. Don't tell me it's not working again. Oh, God, help me.* "I'm sorry, Mr. Wheeler. I was home last night, but my phone has been giving me trouble lately."

"Better get it fixed, Miss Thomas, or you'll lose your customers. At any rate, I'm sorry to have to inform you that I must postpone the presentation."

"Postpone the presentation," she repeated. *No! You mean I dragged all my stuff here, got everything ready, even had an anxiety attack, only to find out I'm not even doing the presentation?* She swallowed the rising indignation in her throat. After all it was her fault. He had tried to warn her last night about the change in plans. Now half the day was shot because of a phone malfunction.

"Can you?"

She stared at him blankly. "Can I what?"

Jeff Wheeler's blue eyes snapped at her like angry waves of the ocean. "Can you do it next Tuesday?"

Lindsay set down the crate with shaky hands, realizing this man and his project had worn down her nerves to frayed bits of wire. She leafed through her briefcase, trying to find her personal data assistant, which seemed to have vanished into thin air. Frustration and embarrassment began to build. Normally calm and confident, Lindsay felt as if the wind had been let out of her sails, leaving her adrift. "I'll have to call you, Mr. Wheeler, and figure out a time that will work."

"It has to be next Tuesday." He nodded and whirled on one foot, giving the impression of a principal who had just reprimanded a student.

Lindsay huffed, heaving a huge duffel bag full of prizes over one shoulder. With both hands, she picked up the crate, the briefcase balanced on top. She crawled down the hallway to her car, wondering what she would do now.

Suddenly the prize bag slipped off her shoulder. The crate fell from her hands, throwing her briefcase off and scattering brochure packets. The duffel bag also fell with a clunk to the floor, accompanied by the sound of breaking plastic.

"Oh, no!" she cried, opening the bag to check the damage. The phone had broken, with Goofy's head now resting at the bottom of the bag. What else can go wrong today?

"Can we help?" came a pair of voices.

Lindsay glanced up to find two high school students staring down at her with large eyes. Instantly, they placed their textbooks and notebooks on the linoleum floor and helped her retrieve the brochures that had skated down the hall in their plastic shrink-wrap.

"Thanks so much," Lindsay said, stacking the brochures back into the crate.

"Are you selling something?" asked the young woman.

"I do fund-raising," Lindsay said, brushing back a tendril of brown hair that had fallen across her face. "I was supposed to start the junior class fund-raiser today."

The students looked at each other. "Hey, we're in the junior class. We were told about the fund-raising project in Mr. Wheeler's history class."

You mean he actually mentioned it? Lindsay then recalled Jeff Wheeler's dream of promoting history activities in the school if he succeeded in impressing his fellow teachers with a knockout sale. No doubt he needed the project to go as well as she did.

"Yeah, we were kind of surprised when they cancelled the assembly," remarked the young woman. "Mr. Wheeler said it had to do with Mrs. Coates. They couldn't do it today because it would interfere with Mrs. Coates's English class."

"Not that we care," added the young man. "We were in for this big vocab test. I didn't even study for it. Did you, Jewel?"

"Not me," said Jewel. "I had that science test to study for. I didn't have time earlier in the week because Mr. Wheeler had us write a paragraph about a cause of the Revolutionary War. I wrote about the proposition that all men are created equal."

"And I told you that's from the Gettysburg Address during the Civil War!" exclaimed the young man. " 'No taxation without representation' is a quote from the Revolutionary War period."

Jewel turned to Lindsay. "You see why I hang around with Troy? He knows history better than anyone. He's Mr. Wheeler's favorite student."

"If you studied more, you'd be the favorite," Troy said. "History is fascinating."

Lindsay listened to the exchange with interest, despite the fact that more precious minutes were ticking away from her business day. *Favored student status, eh?* Perhaps God was smiling on her after all, despite the postponed project and the splintered Goofy phone. "Say, Troy?"

"Yeah?"

"When I kick off this fund-raiser next week, I'm going to need some help. Care to be my assistant?"

"Sure!" he said enthusiastically. "What do I have to do?"

"I'll let you know when the time comes. I think it would be good for the morale of the class, and for your teacher, if a student were helping out with the fund-raiser."

"Can I help too?" Jewel inquired; her large, expressive green eyes reminded Lindsay of her birthstone, emerald. "We kind of do things together."

Lindsay could plainly see the attraction between the two. They were likely boyfriend and girlfriend. "Sure, you can help." She took a notepad out of her briefcase and scribbled out their names, along with a brief description of each. Troy— a long-legged guy with brown hair and freckles, teacher's pet. Girlfriend Jewel—green eyes and curly brown hair, only up to his elbow in height. "Got you down on my list. Mr. Wheeler and I have to settle on a date for the assembly. When you find out from him when it is, come to the auditorium on that day. I'll be setting up a table near the stage. I'll need you to help me form teams among the students. You both can be captains and pick students to be part of your team."

"Great!" they said together with smiles erupting on their faces.

"I hope we make tons of money with this," Jewel commented. "Troy and I are really looking forward to going to the junior prom."

Lindsay watched them touch hands and smile at each other. While she once entertained thoughts of love as a young person, she realized now the dangers that followed those who tripped on emotions at a youthful age. Jewel and Troy seemed sweet and innocent. She hoped they would not hurt themselves by overstepping the boundary. "As long as you're here, how about helping me carry these bags out to the car?"

Each student obliged. One carried the prize bag, the other the crate. Lindsay managed her briefcase. "Thanks a bunch," she said when they arrived at her compact car parked in the circular drive before the school.

"See you at the assembly!" they called.

Lindsay smiled before blowing out a sigh. At least she was grateful for something after wasting half a day. She had a miraculous run-in with one of Jeff Wheeler's pets—a student who loved history as he did. With young Troy assisting her, she couldn't help but get on Jeff's good side and run a better program. "Thank You, God."

Lindsay made it through a day of making sales calls and meeting teachers before driving home. Nestled in a folder on the passenger seat were two more contracts with teachers eager to raise money. Despite the bad start to the day, the rest had gone well. And to think, she now had an excellent way to win over Jeff Wheeler after gaining Troy's help with the junior class project. This might turn out to be one of her more profitable fund-raisers, despite its precarious beginning. The thought excited her.

When she arrived home, Lindsay opened her bag and took out the Goofy phone damaged from the fall earlier that day. She sighed, realizing how costly this was to her presentation. Goofy had captured the attention of hundreds of students with his automated head that lifted when the phone rang, alerting the owner to the call. She simply must have a working model in time for the junior class presentation. Lindsay rubbed her chin until she thought of a fellow fund-raiser in the next territory. Skip Grearson would help her out if he didn't need his own Goofy phone for a presentation. Often, Skip and she would mail each other sales brochures if one of them ran short for a project.

"So you need Goofy," Skip said when she called. "No problem. No, Katy, she doesn't mean Mr. Goofy. I'm talking about the Goofy phone, the one Daddy uses in his work."

Lindsay laughed when she heard Skip explaining to his five-year-old daughter that she didn't need a favorite stuffed animal named Mr. Goofy. Lindsay once took a tour of the Grearson home and was introduced to Katy's vast stuffed animal collection, which filled her entire bed. Lindsay wondered where the little girl slept. She then had the tour of the playroom and indulged in Katy's favorite meal cooked in her play kitchen—plastic eggs, sunny-side up, balanced on a small plate, accompanied by a hunk of fake chocolate cake. "Yes, please tell her I'm not asking for one of her many stuffed friends," Lindsay told Skip with a chuckle.

"So you want me to send it by bus? It will get there tomorrow at noon."

"That would be great. With this sponsor, I'll need all the

help I can get. Maybe the Goofy phone will help lighten him up a little."

"Tough one, eh?"

"The kind that dislikes anything to do with fund-raising. Then he gives me the ultimatum. If this program is a bust, he'll blame me and me alone. Don't you just love it?"

"That's when you need Hank's input."

Lindsay sighed. "Don't I wish." Hank was their territorial manager who came several times a year to watch them start fund-raising projects. He offered advice for making profitable programs and dealing with troublesome sponsors like Jeff Wheeler. "I should call him out here, but then it will look as if I'm incompetent. No, I'm going after this, Skip. After some easy programs, I need a challenge. And Jeff Wheeler's junior class fund-raiser is my challenge of the semester."

"Then go for it. I'll get the Goofy phone out to you."

"Thanks again. And give Katy a hug for me."

Lindsay put down the phone and sighed, thinking about Skip's family. At times she wished for a family she could call her own. A husband who would sweep her off her feet and little ones to tuck into bed, ready to hear bedtime stories. Occasionally, she would wander the toy aisles in the department store, gazing at the products and figuring out what she would like to buy for a boy or a girl. *Yeah, but you need a guy and marriage to make it all happen,* she'd remind herself. A guy like Ron from her high school days. Lindsay shook her head. Ron was out of the picture. She didn't even have his phone number. Maybe she should scout him out on one of those find-a-lost-classmate Web sites. Knowing her luck, he was probably married with a boatload of kids.

The ringing of the phone made her jump. She picked it up.

"Hello, Lindsay Thomas speaking."

"Ah, I see your phone works, Miss Thomas."

Every nerve stood at attention. Shivers, like spiders, raced down her spine. *This is ridiculous,* she chided herself. *I refuse to let this guy get under my skin. I'm going to be confident and friendly.* "Hello, Mr. Wheeler. I have my organizer right here with the appointment schedule and—"

"Well, all right!" he proclaimed.

Lindsay couldn't tell if he were kidding or being sarcastic. She decided to ignore it and act professional. "You said you wanted to kick off the fund-raiser next week?"

"Tuesday."

Lindsay looked at Tuesday. She already had two starts— one at a day care and one for a music department. "I'm sorry, but next Tuesday is pretty much booked. How about—"

"Tuesday," he repeated. He then added, "Please."

Jeff Wheeler, why are you making my life so difficult? "I'll try to move one of the starts," she said, realizing how much she was going out on a limb for this guy. Maybe intuition was at play—the smell of a huge profit that tingled the neurons. Skip often said Lindsay could predict how well her groups would do better than anyone in the company. And she smelled a strong aroma of profit with Jeff Wheeler's little class, if she could get by all the quirks.

"When will I know?"

"I'll let you know tomorrow. Thank you for your call." Lindsay replaced the receiver and stared at her personal data assistant. *So much for my appointment with the director of Over the Rainbow Day Care. It's now been replaced by Mr. Humbug's junior class.* Lindsay closed her eyes and tapped her heels three times. "Send me to the beach," she said with a smile, before turning to the computer.

While scanning for e-mail messages, she saw a pop-up ad for finding old high school classmates. Again she thought of Ron. Dare she try to discover what had happened to him? So many of her classmates had moved away. Only a few were left in the area, and through the years they had lost touch with each other. Her forefinger responded, clicking the mouse button that sent her to the site. She keyed in her old high school and scanned the list of registered classmates, recognizing several names from long ago. Cassidy Richards, the prom queen. John Evans. Michael Jones. She inhaled a deep breath. Ronald Mackley. There he was, big as life. Lindsay's fingers shook as she searched for his e-mail address, only to find that she must sign into the program and pay a yearly fee to access his portfolio. "Of course," she muttered, reaching for her purse and a credit card. "Nothing's ever free in this world."

At last she accessed his personal database, including his e-mail address. She noticed he still lived out in California. She saw no family data. Her fingers trembled as she typed out a simple e-mail message to him. *I wonder what he'll say,* she thought, clicking the mouse. He was one of a kind in her book back when they were in high school. The two of them were quite popular. Lindsay and Ron often gathered a crowd of schoolmates together for lunch. After-school hangouts at the local diner became a daily routine. And quiet nights on a side road they had come to call Lovers' Lane brought back memories of his sweet kisses. Lindsay sighed. She should never have let him go off to college clear across the country. Either that or she should have followed him to the moon instead of staying here in Dullsville, USA, where nothing exciting ever happened, except for her challenging run-ins with Jeff Wheeler.

Before retiring that night, Lindsay accessed her e-mail to find a note waiting for her.

Hey, there!

Great hearing from you. Wow, has it been eight years already? Hard to believe. Glad to see you're doing what you do best, making other people happy by raising them a bunch of money. I've got a great job here at a computer firm. Haven't been back East much, but I hope to someday.

Sure, I remember high school and you. That was a great time. Lots of fun with the gang.

Gotta run. See you.

Ron

Lindsay blinked. No mention of a family within the context of the reply, but no warmth or personal interest either. She sighed and turned off the computer for the night. She should never have expected a spark after all these years. The flame had long since gone out.

three

After all the planning and anxiety over the presentation, the day of Jeff Wheeler's junior class fund-raiser arrived. Lindsay refused to indulge in a cup of hazelnut coffee as she often did in the morning. She feared an upset stomach with the way her nerves were on edge. Despite the relaxing bubble bath she'd taken last night (she'd taken a similar one last week before the project was postponed), she felt uneasy. Her mind went through the list of materials required for the presentation. If she lacked anything, Mr. Wheeler would be sure to mention her incompetence. She checked her notes on his favorite students, Troy and Jewel. If she could grab them before the program began, it would put her in a better position.

Lindsay arrived at the school with plenty of time to spare. She made several trips to and from the car, carrying in the materials. On the way in with the duffel bag slung over her shoulder, she found Jeff Wheeler standing in the rear of the auditorium. He seemed to be perusing the place like a director scanning a set before a major shoot.

"Good morning, Mr. Wheeler," she greeted him in a bright voice. "Nice day out today, isn't it?"

"The students will be here in about a half hour," he answered. Were his hands shaking, or was it her imagination? "What's that?" He nodded at her duffel bag.

"Sample prizes to show the students. They can earn them if they sell enough items. We talked about it on the phone a

25

few days ago." Lindsay set down the bag and withdrew the Goofy phone, shipped out on the bus from Skip last week. "Now this is a great prize. Let me demonstrate it for you." Lindsay pushed the start button, and Goofy did his thing—first the snoring, then raising his head and announcing the telephone call.

"Are you joking?"

"Isn't it fun?"

"I'm not sure if 'fun' is the word I would use. What else is in there?"

Lindsay almost took out a Silly Slammer but decided he would dislike those as well. Instead, she showed off the more sophisticated prizes: a camera, a hands-free headset—"very popular with cell phones nowadays," she explained to his expressionless face—a CD organizer, a personal radio.

"What these students need is something that stimulates the mind. An encyclopedia set on CD, a museum pass, or a gift certificate for a bookstore. That's the problem with kids nowadays. They waste their brains on Play Stations; then you wonder why they come to school brain-dead."

"Uh. . . ," Lindsay faltered. "We've found that students sell better if they have a goal to reach. And of course you do want them to make money."

He nodded and followed her to the front of the auditorium. "So what's the rest of this stuff?"

At least he's curious, she mused. "Brochures, charts for the teams—"

"Teams? This isn't a sports team, you know. It's the entire junior class."

Lindsay felt her cheeks flush. She cleared her throat. "I know, Mr. Wheeler, but the class will do better if the students divide themselves into teams. Accountability among the students helps them sell more." She paused as his gaze centered on her. He did have the most attractive set of blue eyes, but this was hardly the time to contemplate that. "We find that students are more likely to relate to their peers. In fact, Troy and Jewel will be helping me out with this part." She searched for a positive reaction to this announcement but found none.

"Miss Thomas, all I want you to do is hand out the brochures and tell these kids what they're selling. If you must show those prizes, go ahead. Remember you have only twenty minutes. That's all I can give you."

Lindsay felt herself begin to fume. *Does he really want to earn money? Obviously not, with these kinds of ultimatums. He just wants to have it done with and then blame me if the whole thing fouls up.* She inhaled a deep breath, trying to control her nerves. *Keep cool, Lindsay. Don't let him rattle you. Remember the old adage that the customer's always right.* "Hah, what a joke," she said, then felt warmth spreading over her face when she realized her statement had been audible.

Jeff whirled at the sound, staring as if his eyes would pop out of his head. Without a word, he strode off to the rear of the auditorium.

Lindsay pushed the embarrassing moment aside to set up a display of prizes on a blanket of blue velour with the company logo stamped on it. Afterward, she pulled out a sheet of paper printed with a simple introduction. She hoped Jeff Wheeler would at least provide her a decent introduction before the faces of two hundred students soon to occupy the auditorium seats. With great trepidation, she ventured to the rear of the room where he was busy consulting with another teacher.

"Yes?" he asked, without giving her a glance.

"I wanted to give you this sheet that outlines a suggested opening statement for the fund-raiser. Since the students don't know me from Adam, a good introduction will get their attention."

He took the paper and set it on a seat before resuming his conversation with the teacher. Lindsay managed a lopsided smile before hustling down to the front of the auditorium. The students had begun filing in to take their seats. She put on her best smile for the curious faces arrayed before her. All at once she singled out Troy and Jewel, who marched up front. Hope soared within her. She quickly told them to gather more team leaders together. Lindsay then handed out the team sheets, asking the leaders to pick names for their teams and assign groups of fellow students to be a part.

"Glad you both are here," she added in a low voice to Troy and Jewel. "I really appreciate it."

"Sure," Troy said. "Anything to get us out of class."

"Look—I could use the names of some of your football players and other toughies in the class. Also I could use your support during the presentation. When I ask a question, for example, shout out an enthusiastic response every so often. Be motivated, and that will help a great deal."

"Sure." Troy then rattled off a list of names.

Lindsay nodded in satisfaction. With all that accomplished, she strode to the front of the auditorium to await Jeff Wheeler's introduction. Minutes ticked by. The students became edgy. Several of them walked the aisles, visiting friends. A few shouted at Lindsay, asking her why they were here. Lindsay tried to remain patient, waiting for what seemed like an eternity for Jeff to come out of hibernation.

At last he strode to the front of the auditorium with the

paper in his hand. "Quiet down," he ordered the class. "All right—we're having this special twenty-minute assembly so Miss"—he paused and looked at the sheet—"Miss Thomas here can give her little spiel about what stuff you're going to sell to raise money for the prom. I want everyone to be quiet and give her your undivided attention for twenty minutes. Then it's back to class." Without looking her way, he meandered up the aisle and took a seat.

Lindsay felt like dying on the spot. Obviously the man knew nothing about motivating students, let alone giving her a pinkie of help with the presentation. The apathy would certainly trickle down unless she turned it around quick. Lindsay inhaled a breath of determination.

"I'm sorry I had to take you out of your history class with Mr. Wheeler or any of the other classes you have this period. I know how much you were looking forward to that surprise quiz on the Revolutionary War that Mr. Wheeler planned to spring on you today."

At this, the students ceased in their private conversations and stared at her. Some laughed nervously. Others threw looks to the rear of the auditorium where Jeff Wheeler sat with his arms folded.

Lindsay smiled. She had rescued the students' attention with the carefully choreographed introduction. *Thank You, Lord.* "As you know, we're here to raise three thousand dollars for the prom and other junior class activities. I'm sure you all want to hire the best band for the prom—am I right?"

"You bet!" shouted a rowdy student.

"Only the best for our class," Troy added.

"Good. And since the band has to be hired within the next few months, we need the money now. You want to see one of the hot items you'll be selling?"

"Yeah," came a chorus of voices.

Lindsay reached into a bag tucked behind the display of prizes. "After much thought, I've decided you should sell one of Mr. Wheeler's favorite snack foods, sure to make a hit with your neighbors and friends. And of course Aunt Mabel and Cousin Elroy will want crates of it." Lindsay held up a can of Spam, to the roar of the student body.

She glanced to the rear of the auditorium and saw Jeff Wheeler jump in his seat as if struck by the joke. For an instant, she caught the crook of a smile on his face before he lapsed into his usual grim expression.

A burst of confidence shot through her. Lindsay continued with the presentation. She displayed samples of the merchandise on the brochures and the amount each student was expected to sell by the end of the program. "And for all those that reach their fair share of twelve items by tomorrow, we have a special gift for you. A class T-shirt with a mug shot of Mr. Wheeler printed on it."

The students laughed and turned in the direction of their history teacher. He sat straight up in his seat. Again Lindsay detected the quiver of a chuckle on his lips as if he were trying to stifle a laugh. "Really, though, we have great senior class T-shirts printed in fun colors. Now the main question of the day is: Should we also have the opportunity of earning prizes if we sell enough chocolates to Mom, Grandma, and Cousin Louise?"

Affirmations trumpeted the room.

"You mean, you don't want to raise the money simply out of love for your history teacher? Just think what Mr. Wheeler could do with all the money you bring in. How about brand-new, thousand-page textbooks? Or loads of paper to print up all those quizzes and tests? Maybe even a new video system to watch endless movies on the signing of the Declaration of Independence."

Smiles decorated every face. Lindsay loved the students' reactions to her comments. In many ways she felt like an actress in a stage production, only this was more enjoyable. She entered the next phase of the presentation, the prize program. There she showed off radios, mugs, banks and stuffed animals they could earn. "And I'm sure you football players would just love to cuddle up with a little bear."

Groans met her ears.

"Oh, and I can't forget my furry friends who have something special to say about every subject." Lindsay held up several fur-covered Silly Slammers that shouted humorous sayings when they came in contact with a solid object. "I hear that when you get back to your history class Mr. Wheeler is going to give you that surprise quiz. So what do you think of that, Slammie?"

She threw one of the furry slammers to the ground. An exclamation of "Oh, no!" echoed throughout the auditorium. Lindsay then tossed another Slammer with huge red lips to a muscular boy. The loud noise of a kiss erupted. The students roared with laughter.

"Finally, may I introduce you to my friend Goofy. When you are waiting for a call from that long lost love—Troy and Jewel know what I mean—and the phone rings to announce your dream come true, guess whom you hear instead?" She pressed the start button, and Goofy's voice echoed throughout the auditorium, to the laughter of the student body.

"There you have it, gang! So let's do our share for the senior class and make this the best prom ever in the history of Western High."

A round of applause completed the presentation. Lindsay handed out the brochures to the students who filed past her display, looking over the different prizes they could earn. When the assembly concluded and the students left for their classes, Lindsay busied herself with packing up the prizes. She was pleased with the positive response to the program, despite the rocky beginning.

Jewel strode up to Lindsay after the assembly, a frown etched on her once cheerful face. Lindsay thanked her for her support and offered her a class key chain as a gift, all the while wondering about her sadness.

"Thanks," she said. "I just wish what you said would come true."

Lindsay stepped back, caught off guard by the remark. "What do you mean? I know I joked around a little, but—"

"I mean about Troy calling me and telling me I'm his dream come true. I wish he would."

"Jewel, you're young. There's plenty of time for a relationship. Don't take it too fast."

"We've been friends since grade school. I've loved him for years." She bent her head. Golden-brown ringlets cascaded around her shoulders. "He only thinks of me as a playmate."

Lindsay stood for a moment, still holding a Silly Slammer in one hand, before turning to stuff the item into the duffel bag. "Tell you what? Are you doing anything after school?"

"Just homework. Why?"

"Well, there's that greasy spoon—er, that diner—down on Hickory Street. The one with the big neon sign. Why don't you meet me there after school lets out, and we can talk?"

Jewel lifted her face and stared at Lindsay with her flaming green eyes. "Really? Wow, thanks."

"Sure, no problem. And give this to Troy." Lindsay handed her another key chain before Jewel scurried up the aisle. She watched Troy and Jewel examine their key chains, speaking words she could not hear. Jewel then turned and gave her a smile. Lindsay sighed. There was much more to this job than acting up in front of the student body. Many of these young people needed some single-minded attention. She nodded, excited that God might be able to use her in Jewel's life.

Suddenly, a loud "Ahem" echoed in her ear. Lindsay whirled to find Jeff Wheeler staring down at her with his piercing blue eyes.

"I guess you find it effective to abuse the teacher in your presentation?"

Lindsay sucked in her breath, preparing for an onslaught of harsh words. Instead, she caught a twinkle in his eye. Could the day's start have put a crack in that rock solid heart of his?

"I must say, your presentation was quite unusual. Where do you come up with the punch lines—like selling the can of Spam or the mug shot of me on a T-shirt?" He appeared ready to chuckle out loud but pressed his lips together.

"They teach you different techniques in sales school for getting the students' attention," she said, fumbling to place a leftover packet of team charts back in the crate.

"You seemed to have them eating out of your hand. If I could get that kind of response during my classes, everyone would get A's. Then again history isn't exactly a good time to be a stand-up comedian."

"Maybe that's why I never liked history much." Lindsay felt the heat rise in her cheeks. How could she have made such a comment to a history teacher, and having just kicked off his program too? "That is to say, I didn't have a very good teacher," she added quickly. "He would just stand there in front of the class and read out loud from a textbook. There were no visuals, no guest speakers, no field trips, nothing." She turned and packed up the rest of the crates, feeling warmer by the second. For all she knew, Jeff Wheeler might have a similar teaching style. Two insults in two minutes did not bode well for an already strained customer relationship.

"I like visuals and field trips," he answered, to her relief. "That's why I need this fund-raiser. There's a lot more at stake than just the junior prom, you know. Everything I have planned rests on it." He whistled a sigh that illustrated his desperation.

For the first time, Lindsay could see beyond the hardened image of Jeff Wheeler to a man who had a load of responsibility resting on his shoulders. "Just encourage the students every day in your class, Mr. Wheeler," she said earnestly. "Run the prize program. Phone in your first day's totals, and we'll see if we need to boost the prizes. Keep a thermometer chart as I showed you, and remind them of the project each day."

Without a word, he headed up the aisle and toward the exit. Lindsay stood there, staring at her mountain of stuff, wondering if any of this was worth the effort. Only time would tell.

four

From the dingy exterior to the overgrown bushes, the Hickory Diner was nothing to write home about. Lindsay parked the car across the street from the place and stared at the flashing neon sign that blinked the word *Food*. She chuckled to herself, wondering what else the place would serve if it didn't serve food. She rose out of her car and stuffed the keys inside her purse. Several people shuffled into the establishment where she used to hang out with Ron so long ago. She could still feel the strength of his arms curled around her, cradling her close, as they walked into a place where the smell of oil assaulted their nostrils.

Lindsay walked inside. Little had changed since her high school years. The booths were still the same red plastic, the linoleum floors milky and the countertops even more so. Waitresses, clad in their pressed blue uniforms, shuffled among the customers, carrying trays loaded with food that would turn anyone's thighs into barrels. Lindsay knew she shouldn't order anything, but the large chocolate shake in a frosted glass and the heaping plate of French fries that spilled over onto the tray looked very tempting. She slid into a seat and waited for Jewel.

Along the counter on revolving stools sat customers of various ages, eating their food. One held a huge burger in his hands. Another dipped French fries methodically into a puddle of ketchup on his plate. At the far end, a young woman slurped down a soda while talking furiously to a guy holding another of the diner's famous greasy hamburgers. They all seemed so young to her. Either that or she was getting old. Lindsay shook her head. She was young too. Never been married and, right now, no real love relationship. She had her whole life ahead of her. A mere eight years ago, she would have been the young woman at the counter, talking to the guy holding the hamburger. Ron would turn to her, lower the burger to his plate, and tell her that all her questions would be answered at Lovers' Lane.

"Excuse me? Hello?"

Lindsay looked up from her daydreaming to find a familiar face. His eyes were blue, his face rigid, and his lips pressed together as if in disgust. *Oh, no. It can't be.*

"I can't believe I ran into you. I guess this is my lucky day."

Lindsay gaped at him, unable to believe her ears. She was grateful not to have eaten anything, or it would have lodged in her throat and caused a fit. "Mr. Wheeler!"

"I need more brochures. I ran out of them soon after you left. Most of the students took several."

"I have more in my car." Lindsay rose and headed for the car with Jeff Wheeler trailing behind.

"How long have you been doing this fund-raising bit anyway?" he asked.

"Five years. My car's parked right over there."

"Five years? I never would've guessed it. You seem pretty new at this."

Lindsay fought to keep a retort buried within. Only yesterday she'd received a comment card from a sponsor, praising her abilities as a fund-raiser. *This guy has no idea what he's talking about.* "Actually many of the teachers I work with are quite satisfied with their programs." She poked her head into the back seat of the car and leafed through the paperwork inside the crate.

"To be honest, I'm pretty skeptical about this whole fund-raising deal." He sunk his hands into the pockets of his trousers. "It didn't help that I was duly appointed to the role of sponsor for the junior class, without prior approval. I came walking into school on opening day to find my little ol' name up on the wall, next to a list of duties. 'They'll love you, Wheeler,' the teachers all said to me. 'All you have to do is finance the class prom, which is the high point of the year. Remember that the junior class is responsible for raising the money. You won't have any problem, and it will be fun.'"

I've heard all this before, Lindsay thought, rummaging around for the brochures. Her face began to grow warm when she did not find any in the crate.

Jeff continued. "So I went ahead and held a meeting with the class officers, asking them for ideas about raising money. Of course, I knew absolutely nothing. Teaching American history is what I do best. They recommended I collect dues from every student." He paused.

When Lindsay looked up, he was staring off into space.

"I called an assembly of the entire class, as you did today. I don't mind teaching thirty students at a time, but trying to keep the attention of two hundred is pure insanity. I told them why we needed the money and asked them for dues. Guess what happened?"

I can't begin to imagine. Lindsay groaned silently. "Yes, Mr. Wheeler?" She moved to the rear of the car, hoping she had tucked another packet of brochures beneath the prize bag.

"Thirteen showed up with their class dues. Thirteen out of

two hundred students. I knew right then I needed help raising the money. There you have it." He walked to the rear of the car and peered inside. "Did you find those brochures?"

"I'm sure I have them somewhere." She winced, wishing she had not made the comment audible. She didn't need to display ineptness. She opened the prize bag and tossed toys around, when a loud kissing sound erupted from the Silly Slammer with the huge red lips.

Jeff Wheeler leapt back as if he were struck. Lindsay bit her lip in dismay. If things were not embarrassing enough. . .

At last she found a packet and turned to give it to him, only to find he had retreated down the sidewalk. He shook his head. His fingers dug into his pockets as if he were trying to crawl away inside them.

Oh, no! Lindsay groaned. *Does he honestly think I made the sound?*

"I guess Lady Silly Slammer is up to her old tricks again," she said hastily. She handed him the brochure packet.

"Was that one of your prizes?"

"Yes," she said, adding silently, *You didn't really think I would be making lip noises at you, o toad of Western High?*

He took the packet without a word and spun around on his heel. Lindsay watched him go, amazed by his sudden silence after all the tongue flapping he had done. Why had the sound of kissing from a Silly Slammer caused such a reaction? Surely he didn't think that— *Oh, get it out of your head, Lindsay, ol' girl.*

After she locked the car and headed for the diner, she found Jewel striding up to the restaurant, accompanied by a brawny guy. A large tattoo was prominently displayed on his arm, which he had planted firmly around her. Lindsay squinted, quite certain the guy wasn't Troy. Either that or Troy had eaten spinach for lunch and now sported huge muscles with anchor tattoos, like Popeye the Sailorman.

"Hi, Jewel," Lindsay said with a smile.

"Hey." She tucked a strand of hair behind one ear and slowly slipped out of the guy's grasp. "Robbie, I gotta go."

"See you later, Jewel." He gave her a wink and sauntered off, throwing a notebook in the air. The paper fluttered as it sailed back into his hands. Out of the notebook flew one of the brochures handed out that morning in Lindsay's fundraising presentation. It came to rest in the street.

Lindsay blew out a sigh. There was one less student selling.

She must have exhibited a strange expression on her face, for Jewel shook her head and said, "It's not what you think. Robbie and I are only friends. His mom and my mom work in the same factory, so we all know each other."

"Sure, no problem." *But I can tell you for a fact, that guy is eyeing you the way Brutus did Olive Oyl.*

"Hey, was that Mr. Wheeler I saw standing by your car?" Jewel asked, stepping through the door Lindsay held open. The aroma of fried onions wafted through the air. A waitress hurried by with a huge basket of onion rings like large, golden, earring hoops and a mug of soda.

Lindsay was amazed Jewel could see from that distance, especially while being manhandled by Robbie, a.k.a. Brutus. "He needed more brochures for the sale, which is a good thing. That means the students are enthusiastic." Except for Brutus, who let his brochure fall into the street.

"I'm gonna sell 'til I get that Goofy phone you mentioned. I'm gonna get it, park it right by my bed, and wait for Troy to call and tell me he loves me." Jewel sat down in the seat across from Lindsay. When the waitress came, she gave a long order of food including a chocolate milkshake, a cheeseburger, French fries, and onion rings.

Lindsay swallowed hard, not relishing the idea of having to look for new clothes if she consumed that type of fare. When she noticed Jewel and the waitress both looking at her expectantly, Lindsay forced down all modesty and ordered a milkshake and a plate of fries. Jewel relaxed in her seat and gave a smile. Lindsay chuckled, knowing she was now accepted into the fold, grease and all.

"So did you, Robbie, and Troy all go to the same grade school?" Lindsay asked.

"Yeah, we were all in the same classes. Robbie was a bully back then. He picked on Troy all the time. He called him 'brain.'"

This is turning out to be more like Popeye all the time. Maybe I should have Troy over and make him a spinach quiche to help build up those muscles. Lindsay nearly laughed out loud but managed to choke down the emotion so Jewel wouldn't think she was laughing at her. Girls could be funny that way. Any whisper or laugh could mean someone was talking about them behind their backs. At least Lindsay used to think that way.

"That could be a great compliment if you look at it right," Lindsay said when a tall, frost-covered glass was placed in front of her, brimming with a thick, chocolate milkshake. "I always try to turn things around if I can. Can't let cross words get to me, or I wouldn't go anywhere in life."

Isn't that the truth. She thought how easily she would've thrown in the towel with Jeff Wheeler's program, had it not been for sheer determination. She bent her head and offered a silent prayer, then took a drink through the straw. A cold, creamy sensation slipped down her throat. All at once she was back in the old days with Ron, sharing a single milkshake with two straws and laughing away.

"I just love these shakes," Jewel commented. "Anyway, like I was saying, we all grew up together. Robbie and Troy never got along. I got along with both of them okay."

"Did you ever think that the two of them might be competing for your attention?" Lindsay asked.

A strange look came over Jewel's face.

Lindsay hastily rephrased the statement. "What I mean is, if they both don't get along with each other, but they do get along with you, do you see how that could set up a confrontation?"

Jewel shrugged unconcernedly. "Robbie is just someone I know. Troy is. . .well. . .no one can replace him." She took another long sip on the straw. "Robbie understands."

"I'm not so sure. I don't think either of them understands. Troy might not feel the same way you do. And Robbie would as soon take his place if the opportunity arose."

"Troy will understand, and so will Robbie," Jewel insisted. "I just have to give them time. Guys are slow. They don't get it unless you hit them over the head."

"You also have your whole life ahead of you, Jewel. Don't lose it over one guy. I had a guy I liked in high school. We were in love, or so I thought. When it came time for us to graduate, I realized Ron had made other plans—and they didn't include me."

The waitress came and slid their orders in front of their noses. The mound of French fries reached nearly to Lindsay's chin.

Jewel laughed. "Don't they give you a ton of food here?"

"You're not kidding. I have enough oil here on my plate to lube a car."

Jewel giggled. "So what happened to you and Ron?"

Lindsay tentatively picked up a French fry. Even with the amount of fat and calories she was consuming, that first bite tasted better than anything she had eaten in ages. "He was accepted in a college way out in California. I didn't want him to go. We talked it over. We said we would keep in touch." Lindsay paused. "We never did."

"Really? Wow, that's too bad."

"Yeah, it was real bad. I was heartbroken. I tried writing, but if you haven't figured it out yet, guys don't write letters."

Jewel rolled her eyes. "Tell me about it. I've left a million notes at Troy's locker. He ignores them."

Lindsay took up another French fry. "Anyway, I'm just sharing this with you so you don't get your hopes wrapped up in one guy. You never know who else might come along in your college years. You may end up like we did, with both of you attending colleges across the country and a heart that hurts worse than if you handled a hot iron."

Jewel shook her head. Her curly hair swished around her shoulders. "That won't happen to us." Under her breath she added, "I won't let it happen. Troy and I will make sure we go to the same school. We've talked about going to a community college or something once we graduate."

Lindsay turned her attention to the plate of food resting before her. Life's lessons were important to share, but that's about all she could do, and she knew it. They conversed a while longer about Jewel's topic of interest. Lindsay heard all kinds of good things about Troy, from the way he studied for a test, to the way he wore his hair. Jewel nearly idolized him.

Yet in the back of her mind Lindsay recalled Jewel's complaint that Troy did not share her sentiments. How she wanted to keep this young woman from feeling the pain of a broken relationship. Yet sometimes the best course of action was to let these young people discover for themselves whether the decisions they had made were the right ones.

Lindsay returned home to an answering machine blinking a cheerful pattern of lights. She listened to each call, to find the last one from Jeff Wheeler. He left a lengthy message, informing her she had left behind a prize in the auditorium and would she mind retrieving it. He would have it in his classroom. Lindsay picked up the prize bag and began rummaging around, wondering what prize she could have left. The only thing that came up missing was a key chain, which may have accidentally fallen on the floor. "He can keep it," she declared. *I'm not wasting time or emotional energy facing Jeff Wheeler again, just to pick up a silly key chain.*

All at once the phone rang. "Hello, Lindsay Thomas speaking."

"Miss Thomas, this is Jeff—I mean, Mr. Wheeler."

"Yes, I received your message that I had left an item in the auditorium."

"It's one of those class key chains."

Lindsay could hear the chain jingling over the phone. "Mr. Wheeler, keep it as a prize incentive. Tell the students that whoever sells an additional two items, they can have their names put in for a drawing."

Laughter ricocheted in her ears. Lindsay felt her anger on the rise.

"They don't care about a key chain. Hardly any of them have cars."

"Oh. Well, then, you can keep it. Call it a gift."

She heard his hesitation. "I need to ask you a few questions about the sale. Would you mind stopping over early in the morning before classes begin? I get there around seven. We can go over a few things, and you can pick up your key chain at the same time."

Lindsay pulled out her personal data assistant and checked the appointment schedule. She would have to make this a quick visit. She had a start at eight o'clock sharp on the opposite side of the county. *Great. Jeff Wheeler again succeeds in upsetting my schedule. I sure hope this fund-raising campaign of his pays off, because I'm losing time and money.*

"Can you come?"

"Okay, I'll be there at seven." She nearly told him of the other start she had at eight but, remembering his instability in the past, decided not to bring it up. Still, Lindsay had the distinct impression that something was different about Jeff. She couldn't put her finger on it, but there seemed to be less animosity. Lindsay glanced down at the lady Silly Slammer with the pursed red lips, staring up from the open prize bag. "No way. It couldn't be."

five

Jeff didn't know why he awoke anxious and jittery. The thought of swallowing down a hunk of scratchy toast made him nauseous. He made a cup of coffee and tried reading the newspaper after retrieving it from the doorstep. The words made little sense. He glanced around the duplex he owned and found it in complete disarray. History texts stood stacked like small towers on the floor. Class papers were strewn across the coffee table. Dirty clothes lay in the hall. And two days' worth of dishes filled the sink. Not a pleasant atmosphere, especially if he were ever to entertain some eligible young lady in the near future. Jeff cringed at the mere notion. No women like that existed in his circle of influence. If they did, they were independent and single-minded and refused to gravitate to his lonely field of interest.

The thoughts did little to quell his nerves, especially when he thought of Lindsay Thomas fulfilling the eligibility status. He shook his head. Okay, so he was rattled by the strange sound of kissing emanating from the trunk of her car. *Get it through your thick skull, Jeff. It was a prize and not a symbol of some future event.* Besides, Lindsay most certainly had a boyfriend. She was that type—outgoing, friendly, attractive, with shoulder-length brown hair and brown eyes to match. She was dating someone, no doubt about it. He was just plain, ordinary Jeff, the history teacher. She had made it crystal clear that history belonged in a Dumpster and not in her curio cabinet.

Jeff swallowed down the rest of his coffee and grabbed his leather briefcase, stuffed to the gills with books and paperwork. His thoughts shifted to the day's lesson plan—a lecture about the Constitution—and the field trip he had planned with some of his brighter students this coming Saturday. In an afterthought, he grabbed the Christian tour guide that outlined the many monuments and other areas of historical interest in Washington, D.C. The idea of leading the students on a tour and pointing out the nation's Christian heritage excited him. He discovered in the course of his readings how many of the glistening white marbled edifices heralded Scriptures or acclamations of God. In a nation where the news daily batted around the question of separation of church and state, the city of Washington, D.C., proclaimed God on nearly every governmental building and monument. This was what he wanted to show the students—God's hand on a country, even if he wasn't allowed to expound on that fact in a public school classroom.

Jeff winced, thinking of the teacher who had accosted him that one morning while he read his Bible in the lounge. Then he smiled. There were other ways around the issues that divided people. And with God's help he would teach the students not only historical facts, but also of the One who made it all happen.

Arriving at school, Jeff decided to forego the donut and coffee break in the lounge and head straight for his classroom. The schoolroom was his sanctuary, a place where his enthusiasm for history pierced the minds of the young. The huge chalkboard still had the homework assignment etched on it. He wondered how many of the students had read about the Constitution in their textbooks last evening. He knew what they were thinking. Why bother learning about a document written eons ago? If only they could understand that their very rights as citizens of the United States stemmed from that important piece of parchment. Perhaps he could think of ways to stimulate their need to understand the document and history itself.

A faint knock sounded on the door. Jeff turned to find an attractive woman standing in the doorway, outfitted in a black pantsuit, holding a briefcase in her hand. Lindsay Thomas looked stunning, as if she had just walked off the front cover of some beauty magazine. Her brown hair reflected a myriad of gold and auburn tones in the classroom lights. He saw her shift the briefcase from one hand to the other. He had come face to face with Miss America.

"Good morning, Mr. Wheeler," Lindsay announced. "You said you had some questions about the fund-raiser?"

For a moment he couldn't speak. He saw her shift the bag again. The gaze of her liquid brown eyes averted to the chalk-board before settling back on him.

"Yes, I do. Come and sit down." He presented her with a chair.

Lindsay strode over and took a seat. She checked her watch.

Business all the way, he thought. *What does she do for fun, I wonder? Does she like touring museums? Visiting a battlefield? Reading books in the special collections section of the university library?* He shook his head. No, those were the things he liked to do. She probably enjoyed having her nails done, sitting by a pool, or shopping at the mall. At least that's what Jeff's older sister, Candy, liked to do.

"I see you have the thermometer chart up," Lindsay noted.

"Good. This will help the students remember their goal and how much they need to sell to reach that goal. Today you should find out the first day's totals. This will give us an idea of how to proceed."

Her business-like attitude grated on him. If he could only find out more about the flesh-and-bone woman existing beneath the cold business attire. "What exactly do you mean?"

"I mean, if we need to give the students further incentives to sell more. After a few days they start to slow down. You want to keep the momentum going. When the weekend rolls around, you also want them to sell to church people, relatives, and so on." She opened her leather briefcase and pulled out a stack of small cards. "This is where cash cards come in handy. I'll leave a packet with you to show the students when they come to class."

Jeff reached for the cards. Lindsay's fingers were long and slender with nails painted a juicy, ripe plum. Several rings dotted those fingers, but no sign of a diamond. Her fingers trembled slightly as they brushed his, or maybe it was his imagination. "What are these again?"

"Cash cards. If the students sell five or more items over the weekend, they get one of these cards to scratch for cash. The cards come in various amounts—one dollar, two dollars, five, ten, twenty-five, up to one hundred dollars. Because this is an incentive, the teacher pays for this part of the program."

Jeff raised an eyebrow. "I don't know if I like this idea, Miss Thomas. First you want kids to gamble, which really goes against my beliefs. Then you expect me to cut into my profit to pay for it."

He watched a slow flush crawl into her cheeks. The defensive shields went up quicker than a galactic star fighter. "Mr.

Wheeler, this is not gambling. Gambling is when you waste money on a game of chance. This is simply providing the students with a personal goal. They'll work harder if they have the opportunity of winning cash for themselves. Let's face it— we all need a push sometimes to work harder. We do better when we feel we are striving for something."

"Well, their goal is the junior prom, not extra cash in their wallets. If they don't meet it, they don't have a dance. It's pretty simple."

Lindsay picked up the cards and put them in her briefcase. She stood to her feet. "I'm sorry I suggested this. I don't agree with gambling, either, but I think of this as a paycheck for a job well done. If they sell well, they earn something in return."

Jeff frowned over the way this meeting was turning out. Not only had he rattled her, but he found himself turning edgy as well. He stood, reached out a hand, and touched Lindsay's arm. She spun in his direction, with a look of surprise on her face. "I know I don't have the expertise you do. If you think this will help them sell more, then we'll do it. I want this project to succeed."

The jagged lines creasing her face softened at once. Her hand dug into the briefcase and withdrew the cards. The trembling fingers returned. "So you want them?"

"Sure." He took the cards. All at once the door to his room banged open, accompanied by loud voices. Jeff's star pupil, Troy, walked in, followed by Jewel, who trailed him like a puppy dog.

"Hey," Troy said easily.

"Oh, it's Miss Thomas!" Jewel exclaimed. "We went to the Hickory Diner yesterday, Troy, and had a great time. I never knew teachers could be sweet."

"Yeah, maybe you ought to have her be a chaperone on the trip, Mr. Wheeler."

Jeff blinked, realizing what Troy was referring to—the trip to Washington, D.C., this weekend when he planned to take ten of his star history pupils on a tour of the sites. He'd mentioned to Troy his desire for finding one other adult to accompany them, for the safety of the group. He had asked several teachers but found none available. "I'm sure Miss Thomas has other plans."

"You don't have other plans, do you, Miss Thomas?" Jewel asked. "I think it would be sweet for you to come along. We're gonna have a great time. How about it?"

Jeff waited for a look of consternation to form on Lindsay's sleek face at this sudden invitation. He stood there, counting to five, anticipating the certain no, she had a dinner date that night with handsome Harry or a hair appointment at the salon.

"I haven't been to D.C. since I was little. If it's okay with your teacher—"

Jeff nearly fell over. His knees began to wobble. He grabbed the corner of his desk to steady himself.

"Of course it's okay with Mr. Wheeler, right?"

"Sure," he croaked.

Lindsay went over to Jewel and began talking with her in a hushed voice. Jeff observed the interaction between the two. He couldn't help but marvel how Lindsay integrated with the students, much in the same way she'd captured their attention that day in the auditorium. Maybe she wasn't all Goofy phones and Silly Slammers, business and boyfriends. Maybe there was more to her than met the eye.

Later that night Lindsay called Jeff to discuss the students' reaction to the cards. After she slogged her way through the sales pitch, explaining how effective the cards would be in motivating the students to sell over the weekend, he waited for the other items on her agenda.

"Oh, and about the trip this weekend to Washington, D.C."

Here it comes. She has a list of ideas for running the trip, like she did the fund-raiser, as if she has the history degree.

"I will totally understand if you don't think it's appropriate for me to go," she began. "I realize I'm not on the school faculty. In fact, it's probably better if you had a fellow teacher go instead. Or maybe a parent."

Jeff had been all set to remind her this was his trip and he knew exactly what to do and where to go. Instead, her innocent inquiry caught him off guard. No other teachers were interested in participating. No one in high school liked American history that much. The teachers were more into ancient civilizations and European history. At times, Jeff felt out of place talking with them. He recalled one debate with a teacher who passionately pleaded the cause of England during the American Revolution. Jeff countered the statements with patriotic quotes, using documents to support his claims. The debate grew quite hot until Jeff inquired if the man's relatives had Loyalist leanings. That comment drew a look of hostility and a slammed door in his face.

"Mr. Wheeler?"

"There isn't anyone else. The teachers are busy, and I never asked any of the parents. If you want to go, that's fine with me, but I thought you disliked history."

"I do if I have to sit at a desk and listen to a teacher read out of a textbook. I like taking trips, though. I guess I'd better like it with all the traveling I do for my job."

"So you don't work only in this area?"

"Oh, no. My sales territory spans six counties. It seems as if I spend more time in my car driving to appointments than at the schools conducting business. Not to say I don't like to drive, because I do. Sometimes, though, I wouldn't mind if all my schools were just around the corner. Then I wouldn't have to leave the house at six A.M. before the sun is even up. In the winter, I have to get up while it's still dark out. I don't arrive home until after dark."

"Must be difficult."

"It's not too bad. So what time shall we meet?"

"We're meeting at the school at eight A.M. sharp. We're taking a school van up to D.C. It takes about two hours to get there. Be sure you bring money for food and souvenirs, a notebook, permission slip—" He felt the heat rise in his face. "Sorry. I'm used to telling the students what they need to bring."

"I'll take that as a compliment. All right—eight A.M. sharp. See you then."

The dial tone buzzed. Jeff wondered what she meant by taking his blunder as a compliment. Did she mean her age? She shouldn't feel old, that's for certain. She had a youthful vitality about her, especially when it came to giving presentations in front of the students. Maybe it was part of the female psyche, worrying about gray hair and wrinkles. His sister, Candy, worried about it all the time. He recalled Candy finding a gray hair at age sixteen and pleading with him to pull it out.

"Are you crazy?" he told her. "You want me to pull out your gray hair? If I pulled out all of Grandma's gray hair, she'd be bald."

"I'm too young to have gray hair. Just do it." Candy scrunched her eyes shut and waited. He did what she wanted and gave a yank. She then examined the strand like a biologist, comparing it to her natural hair, before tossing it aside.

Lindsay, however, had thick brown hair with a bit of wave, a smooth face without blemishes and expressive fudge-brownie eyes that always seemed happy, no matter what the situation. Jeff shook his head. He shouldn't be dwelling on Lindsay. They had nothing in common. They were like oil and water, night and day, canines to felines. She was a fund-raiser who disliked history but needed work, and he was a history teacher with no money who needed to raise some real quickly. They only needed each other out of necessity and nothing more.

six

Lindsay arrived on schedule at the school, wondering why she'd agreed to accompany Jeff Wheeler anywhere, especially on an all-day field trip to Washington, D.C. She swung a bag over her shoulder that contained a camera, a bottle of spring water, and several granola bars. That morning she'd prayed long and hard for the patience to put up with whatever zoomed out of Jeff's mouth. There was no telling what he might say. She only hoped he wouldn't ridicule her for her lack of intelligence in the area of history.

She never told him her grade in school on the subject, low enough that her parents docked her allowance and made her take summer school. History was boring to Lindsay. Who cared about names, dates, and facts concerning people who were dead and buried? Sure, they accomplished great things in starting the United States, but it made little sense to rehash it all now. Lindsay's number one goal on this trip was to spend time with Jewel and the other students amid the tall, white marbled monuments and buildings. Her agenda was people, not history.

Jeff was already there at the school when Lindsay arrived. He sat on a bench, studying a tour book of Washington, D.C. He never looked up but jotted down notes on a notepad. She stood by patiently, curious to know if he planned to outline his expectations for this trip. Finally, she ventured forward and issued a pleasant good morning, hoping to get the day off on the right foot.

"Morning," he said quickly.

Lindsay shifted the bag to the other shoulder and felt her knees begin to waver. She steadied her voice. "I was just wondering what my duties for the trip will be, Mr. Wheeler."

At last he peered up at her with those same blue eyes that had captivated her in other meetings. In a way, his eyes seemed sad. Her mother often said that eyes could tell a great deal about people—if they were sick or if they were going through a difficult time. She called them the gateway to people's souls. Perhaps those intense blue eyes were doors to some sadness buried away within Jeff Wheeler.

"You can call me Jeff. Just keep the class together. Don't let the students stray. If they have needs or want to see something, then bring it to my attention." He returned to the book.

Lindsay stepped closer to catch a glimpse of the title. In God We Trust Tour Guide. She stood back with a start. Why would a history teacher be studying a Christian tour book? Could it be that Jeff Wheeler was a Christian?

"No way," she said out loud.

The comment drew a puzzled look from him. "Excuse me?"

"Uh, I was—I was curious about the book you're reading."

"We're going to use it to help navigate us through the sites in Washington, D.C. It has some great facts in it. Take this, for instance. Did you know the aluminum tip on top of the capstone on the Washington Monument has the words Laus Deo inscribed on it? It means Praise Be to God. Yes, and it's right on the Washington Monument, the tallest masonry structure in the world."

"I didn't know that."

"Nobody does. All the monuments speak about God.

Everyone is so interested in taking God out of schools and out of our communities that they don't realize there are monuments and sculptures with religious sayings all over them, right in the heart of our government. What are they going to do? Tear down the monuments? Shred the documents that served as the foundation for who we are today? Erase it all and pretend our Christian roots never existed?"

Lindsay fiddled with the strap to her bag. She had little doubt now that Jeff was a Christian, and a devout one at that. Why then had he been so obstinate with her during the fundraising program? *Well, Lindsay, ol' girl, are you perfect yet? Did you ever stop to think there might be more to Jeff than his gruff exterior?*

"That's a good point," she managed to say. "And our currency even says 'In God We Trust' on it."

"That was added during the Civil War. An appropriate time, don't you think—our country embroiled in the worst war known to mankind, with brother slaying brother."

He shut his book in an instant and glanced up. Several cars pulled into the school parking lot. Students poured out of them, smiling and talking with each other, excited about the day they were going to spend in the nation's capital. Troy and Jewel came forward, talking in heightened voices about the time as young kids they had toured Washington, D.C. They mentioned how the buildings seemed like something out of a fairy tale, with gleaming snow-white structures hovering above them, and then their awe at seeing the famous residence of the president of the United States.

Lindsay examined the makeup of the group with curiosity. Four guys and five girls. A manageable number from what she could determine. Nothing like handling hundreds of students in a fund-raising assembly and trying to keep their attention at the same time.

All at once, a burly student rode up on a mountain bike, performed a wheelie and brought the bike to a screeching halt in front of the group. Lindsay couldn't help but gape at the new arrival. The student was none other than Robbie, the one she had nicknamed Brutus for his muscular build and temperament like the villain in the cartoon Popeye. He parked the bike in the rack, chained it, and strode over.

"I don't have you down for this trip, Robbie," Jeff said.

"Yeah, I just found out about it." His gaze darted to where Jewel and Troy were standing. "I love history, Mr. Wheeler. I'd sure like to go if you have the room."

"We did have a student call in sick. If you want to go. . ."

Lindsay could see the distress contorting Jewel's youthful face. "Are you sure you want to do that?" Lindsay said to Robbie. Both Jeff and Robbie whirled to face her. "We're just going to see dumb monuments and boring paintings. Cultural stuff, you know."

"Miss Thomas—" Jeff started, the anger evident in his voice.

Lindsay ignored him. "Besides, I hear they're having some kind of sporting contest in the park today. The Fall Fling. Looks as if you might walk away with the grand prize, Robbie, if you head over there."

Robbie glanced at Jewel who began twisting a small curl of hair around one finger. "Naw, I want to come."

Lindsay frowned. Obviously, the guy had one particular monument in mind, and it wasn't made of stone.

Jeff ushered the students into the awaiting van. While they were settling in, he faced Lindsay. His blue eyes snapped like the flame erupting on a propane burner. "I hope the kind of advice you're giving out today is not what I have to look forward to on this trip. I want my class excited about where we're going. You're telling them it's going to be boring."

"I didn't want Brutus tagging along," she whispered fiercely. "That's all."

"Brutus? What are you talking about? Who's Brutus?"

"Call it woman's intuition, but I think you're making a mistake by inviting Robbie on the trip."

"What? Ridiculous." He stole a glance inside the van. The students sat in their seats, waiting for the trip to commence. Robbie, a.k.a. Brutus, sat in his own seat in the rear of the van with an expectant look on his face.

"Come on," Jeff told her, frowning. "We have a long way to go."

Lindsay took a seat beside Jewel while offering the front passenger seat to Troy. "That way you guys can discuss history," she said. Jewel seemed disappointed by the arrangement but said nothing. Along the way Lindsay tried to make small talk with her, but it was clear she wanted Troy beside her on every part of the trip. In the rear of the van, Robbie cast furtive glances in her direction. No doubt he was itching to occupy the seat Lindsay held. *This is like a three-ring circus, she mused. Everyone is trying to get in on the act. I only pray that everything comes out right in the end.*

ҙ

Sleek, marble structures loomed above the school group when they emerged from the subway tunnel deep beneath the city of Washington, D.C. Students jabbered away with each other while Jeff scanned a map of the city.

Lindsay gazed in awe at the immense buildings towering above her. Being country bred, she rarely ventured into the city realms. The fast-paced life, coupled with untold dangers lurking in every corner, kept her away. She sucked in the exhaust fumes of passing cars. The music of city life filled the air, with horns tooting from impatient drivers, accompanied by the loud rumble of construction equipment.

A student quipped that Washington, D.C., was forever building and refurbishing. Many of the museums had received face-lifts in recent years. Lindsay overheard Jeff say they would be unable to tour the National Archives because of its impending renovation project. "And that means we can't see the Declaration of Independence or the Constitution," he had moaned in dismay.

"All right, everyone. It's several blocks to the Library of Congress." Jeff proceeded in the direction of the building, followed by the flock of students, with Lindsay in the middle of the group. He pointed out the buildings they passed along the way, including the governmental offices. On the left rose the Capitol dome with Lady Liberty perched on top.

"Will we see the Capitol?" Lindsay asked Jewel.

"Of course. The Capitol is one of Mr. Wheeler's favorite places."

"I notice he's carrying a tour book. Guess that will tell us everything we need to know."

"It's one of those religious tour books," Troy pointed out. "I don't know why Mr. Wheeler has to use it. I found him a bunch of good stuff over the Internet, but he still brings that thing along."

Lindsay raised an eyebrow at Troy's obvious disdain for the guide. "I'm sure it's very good and probably quite accurate."

His feet scuffed the sidewalk. "Yeah, but who cares that the buildings have stuff about God on them? I don't believe there's a God anyway. This world is too messed up. When you see all the problems in the world—the terrorism, the wars, kids getting beat up or murdered—I don't understand why a God would allow it to happen and not do anything about it. Either God doesn't exist, or He doesn't care."

Lindsay gave a quick glance at Jewel who remained quiet. Did she feel the same way? "I know there's a God, Troy. I don't know why He lets evil run its course in this world, but I do know He cares about us. And it's obvious the people who came to this country believed in Him too. Mr. Wheeler told me that way on top of the Washington Monument," she paused, turned, and pointed in the direction of the slim monument reaching to the clear blue sky above, "there's a saying that proclaims God. Somebody believed He exists, and they wanted that fact shouted to the whole world."

Troy said nothing. Instead he talked to Jewel about the new rock group hitting the top of the charts. Lindsay retreated from them and began praying for Troy, Jewel, and the other students. She prayed that Jeff and she, along with his tour book, might open the students' eyes to see more than just monuments and buildings, but a God who fashioned a nation and cared about them personally.

Lindsay gulped. What was she thinking? Pray that she and Jeff would help these students? *That's crazy. We barely get along.* Yet, from her vantage point, Lindsay could see the blue book Jeff held in his hand, or "the religious tour book," as Troy put it. They did have one thing in common. Christianity. Lindsay decided to put everything else aside and concentrate instead on what the day might bring. *Lord, open these young people's eyes to see You. And if You want to use Jeff and me in the process, please help us get along.*

At last the group entered the large halls comprising the Library of Congress. Lindsay learned of the many books found there, from those written on ancient papyrus to works stored on microform. Jeff appeared animated as he led the group to a large case that held one of only three special Bibles left in the world. Lindsay discovered the Bible to be an original, printed on the famous Gutenberg printing press in Europe. Many of the students crowded around for a look, including Jewel. Robbie was at her side, reading the plaque along with her. Troy stayed in the background, quietly observing the paintings and sculptures. Jeff gave a small lecture to the group about the importance of Johann Gutenberg's invention of the printing press and its ability to print the very first Bibles. This helped spread Christianity throughout Europe.

The group then entered the great hall, decorated in breathtaking mosaic work and statues that gleamed like fine mother-of-pearl. The architecture itself reminded Lindsay of the interior of a fairy-tale castle. If it were not for the trip's importance, she might have imagined herself a princess in a velvet and jeweled gown, waiting on the staircase to meet her prince. Lindsay stared in awe at the surroundings, unaware that the group had left her behind until she heard Jeff's voice calling to her from the staircase above.

"I hope you intend to keep up with us, Miss Thomas. I don't want to have to send the students out searching for you."

Lindsay looked up to find him on the top landing with his hands spread out across the banister, staring down disapprovingly. "Sorry." She mounted the stairs. "I've never seen such a beautiful hall. I'm not much into art, you know, but the mosaics are wonderful. To think that tiny colored tiles were placed in such a fashion to create these pictures. Can you imagine the work that went into them, the care and the precision? It's incredible. And when I think of the time I take to set up a measly fund-raising program—trying to juggle everything so the program comes out right—I think that in itself is a work of art. This, though, is true beauty that goes beyond description."

Jeff stood frozen in place, staring at her with an intensity that sent a chill racing through her. What could his blue eyes be conveying? A simple acknowledgment perhaps? A measure of understanding? Surely they couldn't mean anything else. Lindsay moved off into the museum where the students were looking over John Smith's map of the New World, a rough draft of the Declaration of Independence written in Thomas Jefferson's own hand, Alexander Graham Bell's drawing of the telephone, and other rare documents.

Lindsay then left the fantasy and wonder of the Library of Congress for the United States Capitol. Again, she was amazed by the immensity of the rotunda where she stood. All around the huge circular room were paintings depicting America's roots. Jeff took the students to each painting and explained its significance. Lindsay saw Pocahontas being baptized, the Pilgrims praying before their voyage to Plymouth in the New World, and John Trumbull's famous painting of the Declaration of Independence. At each one, Jeff shared both the historical and religious significance. Lindsay found herself enjoying his teaching style. She wished she had brought along a tape recorder to capture the moment and play it back when she had more time to ponder it all.

"What do you think of having a painting like that in our Capitol?" Lindsay commented to Troy and Jewel who stood off by themselves, examining the painting of the Pilgrims in prayer, with an open Bible before them.

"It belongs in Plymouth where they landed," Troy said.

"I think it shows their reliance on God, don't you? Can you imagine crossing thousands of miles of ocean through storms in some rickety ship, wondering if you would survive?" Lindsay turned. "And over there, those paintings of the Revolutionary War. You were just studying that time period. How do you think brave men went against a great king like the king of England to gain their freedom? You heard what Mr. Wheeler said. They had to put their trust in God. They could do such incredible things because of their faith."

"Yeah, but they did those kinds of things back then," Troy retorted. "They were all Bible thumpers. Nobody does it now."

"I beg to differ," Jeff said, coming up behind them. The threesome whirled at the sound of his voice. "Did you know that here, today, is a chaplain in the Senate who prays before each session? He prays that God will guide the men and women in their decision-making for the sake of the country. Did you know many Bible studies go on in the Capitol? Many individuals in government keep their trust in God, even in a day of modern conveniences." Jeff blew out a sigh. "We have it so easy nowadays. Look at us. We have cars to take us wherever we want to go. We have instant meals. We have fast communications and computers that spit out what we need. We don't even have to pick up a pen anymore. We are a society that doesn't need God because we've built a society based on man. These people," Jeff paused, gesturing to the paintings, "they had nothing but God to help them overcome their problems. God was the very lifeline of their existence."

Lindsay stood still and quiet, amazed by the truth spilling out of Jeff's mouth. It seemed unbelievable that this was the same man who barely offered her an introduction before the school assembly. A new Jeff Wheeler had appeared before her eyes, one who spoke with authority and power. No longer was he a simple history teacher, but a man full of wisdom and a heart for the things of God.

After this, the students toured the rest of the Capitol, including the Senate and House chambers. They made thoughtful observations before heading over to one of the Smithsonian museum cafeterias for lunch.

When Lindsay had selected her lunch, she stood with the tray in her hands, trying to decide where to sit. The students found tables together where they shared about the things happening in their young lives. Jeff sat alone at a far table with his nose buried in the Christian tour guide. Lindsay boldly marched over and placed her club sandwich and spring water opposite him. He peeked over the book with eyes the color of a deep mountain lake. Then he put the book down, bent over his ham sandwich, and began eating.

"Looks like the students want to eat on their own without us adults hanging over them," Lindsay said.

Jeff said nothing. Lindsay offered a silent prayer for her food before looking at her sandwich. She sincerely hoped this wouldn't be one of those luncheons where people sat stone-faced with fidgety fingers, wondering what words to say that would not offend the other person. It reminded her of stuffy get-togethers with relatives at holiday time. She would sit in her fancy dress, waiting for someone to engage her in meaningful conversation. After enduring it all as a youth, Lindsay made it a point to get the conversation going, no matter what.

"That was quite a speech you gave in the rotunda today." She unfolded a napkin and placed it in her lap.

He stiffened at her words.

Oh, no. I've said the wrong thing already, and I've only been seated here one minute.

"If it was meant to be a speech, I would have gone into politics," he said. "It was supposed to be a history lesson."

"I know that. I only meant it was very moving. Did you see how the students hardly even whispered after that?"

Jeff's gaze left her and traveled to the other tables where the students ate their lunches. Lindsay followed his lead to find Jewel and Troy at the table. Robbie sat with them, appearing to monopolize the conversation. Lindsay inhaled a sharp breath. *I'm sure nothing good will come of that meeting.*

Jeff's voice broke the silence. "I feel sorry for a lot of these young people. Many of them have never set foot in a church. Troy tells me his father was a drunk. No wonder they end up the way they do. They try to find what they're looking for in music, relationships, even substance abuse. They don't know that what they're seeking is staring them straight in the face, like the painting of the Pilgrims praying to God before their voyage. You tell them the truth, but it doesn't seem to sink in."

Jeff leaned forward in a move that startled Lindsay. "If only they could look at the paintings in the rotunda and get a vision for themselves. They can reach higher and go further with God on their side. That's what I'm trying to show them, Lindsay, if only they would open their eyes."

Her heart skipped a beat at the sound of her name floating from his lips. It came forth in such tender fashion, as if he truly wanted her to understand the burdens he carried. Perhaps he never had an opportunity to share his vision with anyone.

Jeff sat back abruptly, picked up a straw, and jammed it into the drinking cup. "Well, it doesn't matter. No one wants to hear the truth. The teachers accuse me of mixing religion and a public institution. I have committed the ultimate crime in my profession, indoctrinating students with the Bible. I'm telling them that Someone cares about them. It might actually change them for the better. They say it's the worst thing I can possibly do."

Lindsay chuckled at the sarcasm in his voice. His gaze fell on her face. "The Bible has become pretty dangerous these days," she agreed. "No wonder Scripture speaks of the Word as sharper than a two-edged sword. It's just a book; yet no one dares come near it. It must be a powerful tool, simply by the negative reaction you receive."

His blue eyes misted over, like a fog muting a once brilliant autumn sky. "You do understand, don't you? I had a feeling you did. I heard you talking to Troy and Jewel in front of the Pilgrim painting. I knew you had to be a Christian."

"Yes to understanding Christianity, but if you mean history, I know nothing. I'm learning more on this trip than I ever did in four years of high school history. I wish you could have taken all your classes on this trip. They would have learned a lot."

"I do too. But if the school board were to find out how I'm shoving religion down these students' throats, they would probably throw me out."

"Then why are you doing it with these students in particular?"

"They all love history. Many have shown an interest in possibly becoming history majors in college. I'm showing them another version of history besides the kind I have to follow in the school. I want them to know that a greater hand lies behind all this history. During a lesson about the American Revolution, when I speak about a fog that suddenly overshadows the East River in Manhattan, allowing

General Washington to escape certain destruction, I don't want them to think it was mere luck. I want them to see God's hand in it."

Lindsay chewed thoughtfully on her sandwich, reflecting on Jeff's passion. In a strange way, they were very much alike. She wanted to reach out to the students as much as he did. What a pair they would make. She reached for the bottle of water to ease the tickle in her throat. Jeff Wheeler and her—a pair? Could it be? Or were they more like a sneaker paired with a combat boot?

seven

Jeff sensed a certain glee well up within him, though he tried hard not to show it. The lunch with Lindsay had turned into something far greater than anything he could have hoped or dreamed. No wonder he often heard the adage of not judging a book by its cover. No wonder God admonished His people not to leap to assumptions on a whim. He had leapt to judgments about her before finding out what lay buried beneath the tough, exterior image. He felt a certain relief in discovering another like-minded soul who wanted students to possess a knowledge of God.

He watched Lindsay talk with Jewel during the trip. The two women had begun to forge a bond. The display motivated him to act. While on their way to the next destination, Jeff met up with Troy.

"So do you have any questions about what we've seen so far?"

"Nope."

Jeff raised an eyebrow at Troy's short retort. "None? You mean, if I were to spring a quiz on you about the day's events, you'd pass with flying colors?

"I don't know about that."

Jeff could see an empty expression in the young man's face, as if something troubled him. Did the lectures in the Capitol rattle the young man? Or were there other things at work? From their previous discussions Jeff knew Troy held little reverence for God. The young man waved away religious persuasion, claiming he had no use for some divine being after his drunken father abandoned his mother and younger brothers in their time of need. Troy refused to think God was in control after enduring such pain. Jeff rarely conversed with Troy about religion but decided to use the young man's fascination for history as a vehicle for showing him the reality of God. Despite his efforts, Troy appeared more distant than ever.

Lindsay now moved away from Jewel to interact with the other students. Like a hawk, Jeff watched Robbie swoop down on Jewel and engage her in conversation. When he did, Troy grew rigid. His face turned crimson. He left Jeff's side and strode forward with determined steps toward Robbie.

"Excuse me, but I think you've spent enough time talking to Jewel."

Robbie laughed. "What are you, her big brother? You are, aren't you? Isn't he, Jewel?"

"Robbie, Troy's very special. He's—"

"Sure. A brain on two legs. He's nothing, Jewel. But if you want to talk to him, go right ahead. I won't tell you who you can and can't talk to. Slavery ended a long time ago."

Troy balled one fist. The tension between the two was as tight as a rubber band around a stack of papers. One more episode and it was liable to pop altogether. Jeff saw Lindsay flash him a look, reminding him of the warning she had given that morning concerning Robbie. He sighed, wishing he had listened.

Jeff decided he'd better shift the pent-up energy to the area of knowledge. He began asking the students questions regarding Abraham Lincoln's presidency while they made their way to Ford's Theater, the place where Lincoln was assassinated. Instead, he overheard Jewel and Troy exchanging harsh words about Robbie.

"He's a family friend, Troy," Jewel insisted. "You know our mothers work together."

"Sure. Some friend."

"I didn't know you cared that much."

"I just don't want you hanging around with a loser like him."

Jeff cleared his throat. "So, Troy, tell me in what year the Civil War came to an end."

Jewel and Troy continued their conversation, ignoring Jeff's question. He inhaled a sharp sigh before repeating it. Troy only stared hard between Robbie and Jewel before spouting out, "1865."

"And can anyone tell me what play Lincoln was going to see the night he went to Ford's Theater?"

Another student provided the answer while Troy and Jewel remained engaged in their own personal difficulties. So far, this plan was not easing the tension. Jeff cast a glance at Lindsay. She seemed to understand Jewel. Perhaps she could further enlighten him to the troubles existing between them all. While the students were examining the booth inside Ford's Theater where Lincoln was assassinated, Jeff approached Lindsay. She stood staring at the interior of the theater in obvious fascination when he posed the question.

"Jewel, Troy, and Robbie are in an unpredictable love triangle," she explained. "I warned Jewel this might happen. Both Troy and Robbie are competing for her attention. Jewel really likes Troy and wants him to care about her. She also has an affinity for Robbie who is a childhood friend. Naturally, Troy and Robbie clash."

"I see. So that's why you didn't want Robbie coming along on this trip."

Lindsay scanned a pamphlet about the theater. "I had an inkling something might happen. I take it that interpersonal skills are not your strong point."

"No. If they were, I would probably win Most Popular Teacher. I can teach, but I can't deal with people's hang-ups. Counseling is not a part of my job description."

"But you can't help interacting with these students. As a teacher you must see what some of them have gone through in their lives."

"Sure, but that doesn't mean I know what to say. If I need to, I send them to the school nurse who recommends them for counseling."

"Maybe you teachers need a little counseling too?"

"What's that supposed to mean?"

Her face reddened. She stepped backward into the decorative walls of the old theater. "I mean, you see a lot of what goes on. You have to deal with a lot. It's bound to get to you after a while."

Lindsay didn't know the half of it, but she came pretty close, more than anyone he had ever met. He surmised that her close association with teachers helped her understand their woes. Not only were teachers responsible for learning, but they also had to deal with the problems students brought into the building. It became a never-ending struggle, balancing the art of learning with social behavior.

The group headed downstairs to the museum where Jeff examined the cases of artifacts, along with the students. Looking from the coat Lincoln wore when he suffered the fatal bullet wound to the door that separated the killer from the presidential box, he thought back to the time of Lincoln. Even in those times, deeply disturbed people did terrible things, even going so far as to assassinate one of the most beloved presidential figures in American history. Jeff didn't want to see any students of his turn into evil people. He wanted them to lead productive lives. What could he do? Teachers had no counseling degrees. Perhaps if he continued using history as a mechanism to point them toward God—at least that was a step in the right direction.

While the students gathered in the gift shop to look for a few mementos, Jeff slipped into the men's room. At the sinks, he found Troy and Robbie squaring off. The young men, with red faces and hands clenched into fists, stood before each other, waiting for one or the other to throw the first punch. Jeff swallowed hard when he saw the sight. Breaking up fights was not his forte. Yet he could ill afford a bathroom brawl on a school outing, or the board would never allow him to conduct another field trip in his life.

"All right, guys—what's going on?"

"Nothing." Robbie wiped the sweat off his upper lip.

Troy didn't answer.

"Look—if you guys can't be civilized, then you're going to have to stay away from each other and from Jewel. I can't have this going on. We're here to learn, not to pick fights."

Troy marched off, mumbling something unintelligible under his breath. Robbie shook his head. "I don't know, but Troy really has a problem."

"I doubt you're helping the situation."

"Hey, all I did was talk to Jewel. Troy acts like he owns her. She and I go way back. Our mothers are good friends. He's the one who needs to learn some self-control. Man, he almost landed me one right in the face. I had to duck, you know."

"Then you two had better keep away from each other. I

know you, Robbie. You'll get under people's skin just to irritate them."

"Yeah, and I know Troy is teacher's pet, so that doesn't help me either, does it?"

Jeff felt his vexation rise. He let the comment go and retreated to the museum. Lindsay gave him a questioning glance, but he ignored it.

Shortly thereafter he called it a day and decided to head the group back home. The events had worn him down to the point that he felt like collapsing on the sidewalk beside the homeless people sleeping in the parks of Washington, D.C. Everything seemed in total disarray. Troy and Robbie grated on his nerves like dual food processors. He'd had such high hopes for the trip, too. On the drive home, his thoughts were a puddle of mush. He stayed quiet, even when the group stopped briefly at a fast food restaurant before arriving back at the school.

When the last of the students had been picked up, Jeff dragged himself to his car. In the distance, he saw Lindsay preparing to enter her own vehicle. Perhaps there was one bright spot to this gloomy day. Even though she appeared a bit haggard, Lindsay was still stunning to his beleaguered eyes. Something about her stirred him, especially after their adventure in Washington. He decided to ask her out for a cup of coffee. He needed to brush off his concern over Troy and Robbie on someone. To his relief she agreed to go.

They headed for the closest coffee shop and ordered cappuccinos. The place was nearly deserted at that time of night. Most patrons required coffee in the morning to jump-start their day. Jeff didn't care that the coffee might keep him up all night. He needed this time more than anything right now. He swallowed down half his cappuccino before confiding in Lindsay of the confrontation in the rest room of the museum.

"I thought something like that would happen. Both Troy and Robbie had ugly looks on their faces. They're like gang leaders."

Jeff shivered at the comparison. "I'm not sure what to do. To top it off, Robbie has accused me of showing favoritism. I realize Troy and I have had several conversations. I like to stimulate his interest in history, but I don't want my classes to think I'm showing favoritism. It looks bad, you know."

"I used it to my advantage," Lindsay mused.

Jeff straightened in his seat at these words, wondering what she meant.

"I discovered Troy was a favorite and used it to help with the class fund-raiser." She closed her mouth and bent her head as if embarrassed by the fact.

Jeff chewed on his lower lip. "Then that proves there's a problem."

"It doesn't prove anything. All teachers have favorites when they find students who love their subjects. Besides I wanted your fund-raiser to succeed. I realize how important it is to your future at Western High. That's why I picked Troy to help me."

"I'm trying to teach these young people history, but I guess I'm letting other things get in the way, like showing favoritism. Jesus didn't show anyone favoritism. He wanted everyone to know Him."

"Yes, but the Bible talks about the one disciple Jesus loved. I think sometimes God knits us together with people so we can reach them in a particular way. I believe we've both been drawn to Jewel and Troy for some special purpose. Initially, we may have been drawn by other circumstances. I think now we see that we may be able to help them."

"I still don't want to show partiality or give the appearance of it. This makes the students hostile toward one another, like what I witnessed today."

Lindsay sipped on her coffee. "I wouldn't worry about it. Just do the best job you can with what God gives you. After today I can see He's given you a great gift, Jeff. It's good to see Christian teachers using whatever opportunity they have to share about God. We need more of that in the schools."

"It's not easy, let me tell you. If some teacher thought I was thrusting my religion down students' throats, I could find myself sitting out on a step with an unemployed sign hanging around my neck. It takes wisdom in these kinds of situations."

"Yes," she agreed. "I had a teacher once that I tried to counsel. She was coping with a marriage break-up. I tried to tell her how much God wanted her marriage to work. When she realized what was happening, she blatantly told me not to put my religion on her, especially on school property. I was pretty surprised. She also ended up canceling the contract. It would have been a great program, too."

"So you've had it happen to you."

"Yes. I bawled my eyes out on Skip's shoulder. He's a Christian and understood where I was coming from. He told me I needed wisdom, too. Be wise as serpents and gentle as doves."

Jeff never heard her final statement. He felt as if a sharp needle had suddenly jabbed him. Never mind what they had been discussing, though it was highly important. Right now he could only concentrate on the fact that Lindsay had a boyfriend named Skip. He had just begun working up the courage to ask if she might want to go to a historical site sometime, like Williamsburg or Jamestown. Come to find out, she was already taken. Jeff thrust the coffee down his throat and informed her it was getting late.

During the drive home, he felt empty inside. The whole day seemed like a waste, a day he had planned since the beginning of the school year. The students were mean to each other and disliked him for showing favoritism. And now Lindsay had a boyfriend. What did he have to show for this day except sore feet from traipsing across hard floors and cement sidewalks?

Jeff pulled into the parking space by his duplex, laid his head back against the seat, and closed his eyes. What ever led him to believe he and Lindsay might have something going? At first, everything. Her whole personality; her love for the Lord; her childlike interest in history, like one just discovering a new world; her involvement with the students—it all tugged at him with a force he could not shake. Now that she had a boyfriend, he had nothing to fill the void. He swung the keys around his finger. He would have to go on teaching history to students who cared little about the subject and hope that along the way God might have a few surprises left for him.

Jeff entered the lonely apartment to discover he had left the milk container on the table from breakfast. A disagreeable odor drifted to his nostrils. He poured the remaining contents down the drain and, in that moment, saw his hopes and dreams vanish along with the sour milk. "I should be singing 'and away go troubles down the drain,'" he mumbled to himself, "but there only seem to be more in the works."

He went to his answering machine and found several calls. The last one was from his older sister, Candy. "Hey, little bro, give me a call when you get a chance and let me know what's going on in your life."

Jeff sighed. To Candy he would always be "little bro," no matter what his age might be. Only five years spanned them, but Candy believed she had lived life. At that moment, he didn't care. She might provide the help he needed. He craved advice after a day like today. He picked up the phone to punch in her number. If there were one area Candy had plenty of knowledge, it was relationships. She'd had many in her years, though not in the way Jeff would have envisioned. Still, maybe she had some ideas.

The phone rang six times before a voice answered. Loud music filled the background. Jeff cringed at the rock and roll that attacked his eardrums. "Hey, this is Jeff!" he shouted above the roar.

The music instantly died. "Hey, little bro, what's up?"

Jeff pulled out a chair and threw himself into it. "I need some advice about a certain woman."

"All right! You finally found one. I was worried you'd be a bachelor for the rest of your life."

Jeff said nothing for a moment. Candy's own marriage had collapsed after two years. He had decided he'd rather stay single for as long as needed rather than face the pain of a broken marriage. "I'm not that old. Thirty is hardly old anymore. Besides I want her to be the right one."

"Well, if you're going to make any headway, you have to at least start dating and find out if you're compatible. Have you gone out yet?"

"I don't want to shop around. I'd rather get to know one in particular, maybe over a cup of coffee. In fact, there's a woman I wouldn't mind getting to know, only tonight I discovered she has a boyfriend."

"Okay, so give me the long end of it."

Jeff was thankful Candy had switched off the music so he could hear himself think. He went into the aspects of their relationship during the fund-raiser and the trip to D.C., leaving out most of the religious parts since Candy wasn't a Christian. She listened patiently until he came to the coffee shop scene and Skip's shoulder.

"Are you kidding? You should have still asked her out."

"I can't do that."

"Why not? I mean, she didn't say this Skip was her boyfriend, did she?"

"No, but she cried on his shoulder. What other shoulder would you cry on unless it was a good friend's—or a brother's?" He hinted at their relationship and the times Candy came to him, telling him about the guys who had dumped her. He recalled many a wet shoulder after those encounters. When he'd suggested she forget about relationships for a while and pursue other things, she cried even louder and told him he was insensitive.

"For all you know, Skip could very well be her big brother! You'd better find out what's going on before you start making assumptions. Then make your move."

"Right. Make my move where? The moon?"

"Oh, how romantic. One of those boat rides under the silvery moon. Can't you just see it, Jeff? Really—take her wherever you want. Wine and dine her."

"I don't drink. I prefer coffee."

"Fine, the coffee shop—though that sounds pretty boring to me. Maybe offer to take her someplace she would really like to go. What does she like to do?"

"Uh. . ." He hesitated. What did Lindsay like to do? He

had no idea. All he'd talked about were his interests without bothering to discover hers. Maybe that's why she preferred Skip's shoulder for a good cry. Maybe Skip spent time asking her what she liked in life, and she felt comfortable confiding in him about her woes. Maybe she enjoyed shopping in the mall—like browsing through toy stores, looking for toys to use in her fund-raising presentations. The thought appealed to him. Searching out toys might make him feel young again instead of a stuffy old history teacher who had lost his knack for fun.

"Hey, are you there?"

"Yeah, just thinking. Okay, I'll find out some more details. I just thought after a day like today that there might be something between us. I don't want to lose what's there, no matter how insignificant it may be."

"Then go for it. Let me know what happens."

Jeff hung up the phone, relieved after talking it out with Candy. No longer did he feel sour like the milk he had dumped down the drain. He would find out all he could about Lindsay and see if he had any reason to hope for the future.

eight

Lindsay couldn't believe what she saw on the computer monitor before her. She blinked once, then twice, to make certain she was reading the words and not imagining them.

> *Hey, Lindsay,*
>   *Guess what? I'll be in your neck of the woods tomorrow. The boss wants me to attend a special conference outside Washington, D.C., and he bought me a last-minute plane ticket. Since I knew you were in the area, I jumped at the chance. Maybe we can catch dinner. Let me know your plans and if you're available.*
>
>   *Ron*

Lindsay stared until her eyes began to hurt. *Ron is coming to town, and he wants to see me.* She swallowed hard. Her eyelid developed a nervous twitch. Eight years had passed since they'd seen each other, shortly after receiving their high school diplomas. She recalled a pool party they went to at the parents' of one of Ron's close buddies. They had just finished sharing a kiss inside the cabana when he dropped the bomb, announcing plans to attend college in California. Lindsay felt as if someone had knocked her over the head. He told her he was sorry it wasn't someplace here, but this was a great opportunity to launch himself into a high-tech field in the Silicon Valley. Tears burned her eyes that day.

Her heart felt like a lump of lead. When he left for college, her whole world fell apart.

Now he was coming back. Could she handle such a meeting? Was she ready for something like this after eight years? *You were the one who started it all, Lindsay, ol' girl,* she reminded herself. *You sent him that E-mail, asking him how he was. You might as well have sent an invitation in bold black letters with the words "Here I am! Come and get me!"*

At one time she'd wanted to see if a spark still remained. He had been her first and only love. They had shared so many good times together. *I was a kid back then, and I wasn't a Christian,* Lindsay reasoned. Neither was Ron. *And what if he still isn't? How can I think of rekindling the past with an unbeliever?*

Suddenly she grew nervous at the prospect of a meeting. *I might well be inviting disaster, not to mention the emotional upheaval. I can hardly handle my life as it is right now.*

Turning to the computer, Lindsay typed back a message, informing him she would be too busy but thanked him for the offer. Her finger wavered over the mouse button, uncertain if she wanted to send it. Here was a chance for love to be rekindled. Yet the mere thought of a relationship with Ron made her uneasy. She had no peace. Finally, she hit the mouse button with force, sending the E-mail on its way. *There! It's better this way. Leave the past behind and embrace the future.*

Lindsay was shuffling through the paperwork overflowing on her desk when the phone rang. She answered it in a hurry, knocking over several boxes of chocolates she had stacked on the desk, ready to return to the merchandising department. The corner of one box ripped open, dumping a few heart-shaped chocolates onto the floor.

"Hi, Lindsay. It's Jeff."

"Jeff," she repeated. Jeff who? Her confusion continued for another second or two until it dawned on her that this was Jeff Wheeler, the history teacher from Western High. She straightened in her seat. "Jeff, how are you? I guess you'll find out tomorrow how the sale is going. You're going to do the cash cards with the students, right?" She reached down and picked up the box of chocolate hearts. In an afterthought, she opened the box all the way and popped a piece in her mouth.

"That's the plan. As you said, students love the idea of earning a few extra bucks. I'm expecting to give away most of the cash cards you gave me."

She marveled over his optimism that seemed so uncharacteristic for the man after their past meetings. They had left each other quite abruptly in the coffee shop too, almost as if the conversation had struck him in the wrong way. Lindsay wondered about it the night she got home but couldn't think what it might be. Perhaps he was only tired out, as she'd been. It had been a long day, filled with mixed emotions.

"So where do you go to church?" he asked out of the blue.

Chocolate and caramel swirled together in her mouth. "I go to Covenant down the road from me." She swallowed and stifled a cough when the chocolate tickled her throat. "They have services this evening, too, but I rarely go. Most of the time I have to get ready for starts the next morning."

"Do you have a fund-raiser tomorrow?"

"Yes, as a matter of fact, with the Over the Rainbow Day Care. I'm meeting with the director." She nearly confessed to him that this was the fund-raiser she had to move when he abruptly changed his own start date but decided to omit that fact. "They want to raise money for playground equipment."

"I take it you raise people lots of do-re-mi."

"I try. It's how I get my own do-re-mi to pay the fa-so-la-ti bills."

"Huh? Fasolati bills?"

She laughed outright. His ignorance endeared him to her. "Haven't you ever seen the movie *Sound of Music?* The kids sing 'do-re-mi' followed by 'fa-so-la-ti.'"

"Do you like those kinds of movies?"

"Sure. I grew up with them. I enjoyed skipping down the sidewalk, singing 'do-re-mi.' I also like the song 'My Favorite Things.' 'Raindrops on roses and whiskers on kittens, bright copper kettles and warm woolen mittens—'"

"Hey, you want to rent it and see it sometime?"

Lindsay's skin broke out into goose bumps. Every hair stood at attention. The old eyelid began doing the twitch. "Excuse me?"

"I mean, would you like to come over sometime and watch it? We can order out for a pizza or something, unless you don't like pizza. Maybe even tomorrow night. I'm free."

Lindsay dearly wanted to tap the receiver and ask if this person were actually Jeff Wheeler. The idea he wanted to please her with a movie, and a musical at that, sent questions running through her mind. Had she made that much of an impression on him during the field trip? "I'd like to, Jeff, but that's the night I call teachers for potential fund-raising programs." She heard the audible sigh. "If we make it early, though, I might be able to. Would you like to come here instead? You can pick up the pizza and the movie on the way here. I have an old VCR that still works. We can watch it over dinner. Then I won't have to do much traveling, you know, and I can make my calls afterward."

"Okay. Sounds good." She could hear the excitement in his voice. "I'll let you know tomorrow how the fund-raiser is going and if there's anything else we need to do before it wraps up."

"That would be great." Lindsay hung up, her mind in a whirlwind. *Don't read anything into it,* she cautioned. Yet the idea he wanted to do something besides history made her all the more curious about his intentions. She picked up another chocolate heart and stared at it. The chocolate began to melt from the heat of her fingers. She ate it without a thought to the promise she'd made of not indulging in company sweets.

Why does Jeff want to do this? Maybe he's looking for a history buddy. Lindsay nearly choked on the chocolate and went to the kitchen for a glass of water. History buddy, indeed. She was more like a history baby with her lack of knowledge in the area. To her, April showers brought the Mayflower. Washington was the guy on the dollar bill and, yes, the name of a tall monument in D.C. (She had learned this on Saturday.)

She chuckled, imagining Jeff's reaction if he knew the extent of her historical knowledge. He would likely be horrified. Most of the history she knew had been learned from the tour yesterday. The godly roots in the founding of their nation amazed her. She wondered how many students in the schools really knew about the Pilgrims' devotion to prayer or the baptism of Pocahontas.

Well, it didn't matter. Jeff was bringing her favorite movie, and that's what counted, not her knowledge of history. A pizza and a movie might be just the way to relax after a busy day, without having to delve into topics she knew nothing about. If all else failed, she could dazzle him with her knowledge of the *Sound of Music.*

2&

The appointment with the director of the day care went well, except that Lindsay discovered a grape jelly stain on the elbow of her favorite white blouse when she arrived home. She immediately took it off, threw on a T-shirt and soaked the garment in the bathroom sink with some mild detergent. How was she to know that the table where she sat, discussing project details with the sponsor, was also the same table where the kids ate their peanut butter and jelly sandwiches at snack time?

Lindsay then raced around the apartment, straightening here and there, moving stacks of contracts to her desk and jamming everything else into the office. She struggled with the door, trying to shut it, with several cardboard boxes impeding the effort. The last thing she wanted Jeff to see was her sloppiness. No doubt he expected a woman's habitat to shine. Lindsay dragged out the hand vacuum and went about sucking up month-old crumbs. She straightened the pillows on the sofa, sewn by her mother. A country scene of a farmhouse and cows decorated one pillow, a Noah's Ark scene the other.

She had just scurried back to the bathroom to rinse out the blouse when the doorbell rang. *Oh, great! He's early.* She moaned, staring at her ratty T-shirt. *What am I going to do?* She ran for the bedroom and grabbed the first shirt out of the drawer, throwing it on before dashing for the door.

A tall man stood there, dressed in sharp business attire. Dark brown hair ruffled in the breeze. The strong scent of his cologne made her woozy. Lindsay stared in bewilderment.

"Surprise!"

"Ron? Ron! Oh, no—what are you doing here?"

"Hey, great seeing you too after eight years." He looked miffed.

"How did you know where I—"

"Ever hear of the phone book?"

This can't be happening! "Oh—well, how are you?"

He stared at her rather quizzically. "I'm fine, but what about you? You look like you got up on the wrong side of the bed this morning." His gaze traveled to her clothing before returning to her face.

"Huh?" Lindsay peered down to find lines of sewn material staring up at her. She could feel the heat in her face. I don't believe it. My shirt's inside out.

Ron laughed at her predicament before following her into the small apartment. Lindsay hurried to the bedroom to put the shirt on correctly. When she returned, Ron had made himself comfortable on the sofa, with his head propped up on Noah's Ark. "Nice place. So how are you doing?"

Her heart began to thump. Ron looked better than she ever imagined. Gone were the boyish airs of yesterday. A grown man had taken over, and a handsome one at that. Dark brown hair framed the rigid lines of maturity on a face now absent of freckles. The business clothes made him appear distinguished. She discovered no wedding band on his finger. Single, too. Could that be? *Lindsay, ol' girl, you have Jeff coming in a half hour.* She decided to make this a quick "Hey! How are you? I've got a ton of things to do" meeting. *I won't offer him anything to drink. Drinks add on another thirty minutes. I'll sit quietly for about fifteen minutes then tell him I have work to do.*

Ron opened his mouth and talked nonstop for ten minutes. He told her about his job in California, the great scuba diving in Monterey, and a hiking trip he took in King's Canyon, where he enjoyed the beauty of the Sierra Nevada. His job was next, and the huge income he was making. It was typical male talk—money, mixed with muscle. "So what about you? I hear you're making a little money yourself."

"Little by little." She spoke swiftly about her fund-raising business.

His arm rested across the back of the sofa—the same strong muscular arm that once cradled her close on cool, star-filled nights at Lovers' Lane. She trembled at the thought. No, she did not want his arm around her now. She couldn't. Her life was different now and taking stranger detours every day, it seemed.

"Do you keep up with the old crowd?" Ron asked.

"A few. I see Jessica and Kate occasionally. Everyone else has moved away. You can't blame them. There's not much around here. Did you know they now have a new high school? They built it four years ago."

"So I've seen. High tech. The old building is some kind of institution. Not that we didn't go to one anyway!" His finger traced the edge of the sofa. "I've been thinking about the times we used to have, Lin. Did you know I drove out to Lovers' Lane? Still looks pretty much the same. And there's that spot you used to like, by the old stone wall."

Lindsay felt her cheeks begin to heat up. Her palms started sweating. "Oh, really. I haven't been there since. . ." She gulped and looked away, hoping he wasn't staring at her.

He was, with that misty-eyed, melting look of someone who had not forgotten their encounters back in high school. "Yeah, we spent quite a bit of time there, didn't we?"

This is getting more uncomfortable by the minute. Her stomach began to churn from the tension. Lindsay looked at the clock. Ten minutes to go before Jeff's expected arrival.

"That was a long time ago. We're different people now. We live on opposite sides of the country."

"We're not that different. Besides, I hear that opposites attract. What do you say we grab a bite to eat and go see some of the old places? We can check out where we once went to high school in that place that's now some private institution. Maybe even Lovers' Lane and see if there are any sparks left after all these years." He rose to a towering six feet in stature and stepped toward her. "I have a feeling there might be. You look stunning, Lin, even better than I remember."

Lindsay felt her eyelid begin to twitch again. She could kick herself for looking up his e-mail address and shooting off that initial note. The money she would have saved from joining the classmates Web site might have been better served elsewhere. Now the contact had opened up a can of worms best left hidden in a dark closet and sealed with super glue. *Brilliant work, Lindsay. Dumb is more like it. He really thinks I want us back together.* "Ron. . .I. . .well, as I said in my E-mail, I can't. This is, uh. . .my work night."

"I think you can put it aside for one evening, can't you? I came all the way from California, not to mention nearly blackmailing my boss to get me here. Isn't that worth a night on the town?"

The doorbell rang.

Saved by the bell. *Thank You, Lord.* Lindsay ignored the look on Ron's face and went to answer the door. Jeff stood there with the pizza, a movie and five minutes to spare. She could have kissed his feet for coming to her rescue.

"I hope you don't mind. I came a little early."

"I'm glad you're here." *You don't know how glad.*

Ron came up behind her at that moment. Jeff's face turned

the color of glue. His arm weakened. Lindsay thought he might drop the pizza on the concrete landing.

"Hi, I'm Ron." He offered his hand.

"Jeff." He didn't offer a hand, both of which were occupied by the pizza box and the movie.

"Well, Lindsay, I'd better get going." Ron gave a lopsided smile. "Good seeing you again." He scooted past Lindsay and Jeff and headed for his rental car. The sound of the engine was like a soothing melody in her ears.

For a moment, Lindsay and Jeff stood staring at each other. She could see him calculating the encounter by the way his blue eyes were shifting back and forth, trying to figure out what was going on.

"I didn't know you had company," he finally said.

"It was totally unexpected. Ron is someone I used to know back in high school. He was going to a conference here in town and stopped by."

Jeff nodded. He followed her inside with a hesitation to his step, unlike the confident Ron who had made himself right at home. He stood in the foyer of the apartment, waiting for an invitation, just like a gentleman.

"Make yourself at home," she invited him. "I'll get some plates and drinks."

She returned to find him sitting stiff and straight on the sofa. Gone was the confident history teacher of Western High. In his place was a marble statue, like those found in Washington, D.C. At least his uncertainty eased any misgivings concerning this encounter. He hadn't come here to strong-arm her like Ron. In fact she wondered why he was here in the first place. Maybe he was lonely and in need of a friend. Lindsay knew how that felt. Even though she had grown up in this town, most of her friends had moved away. She still had family around and her church family as well. Yet they all seemed so busy, caught up in their own little world. She was grateful Jeff thought enough to share in a little of her world, even if it was filled with musicals and visions of fairy tales from long ago.

And little did he know, but he had also rescued her from what might have been a very bad evening.

nine

The pizza was just the way Jeff liked it, coated with pepperoni and stringy mozzarella, yet he hardly tasted any of it. Ever since he'd stepped inside Lindsay's house, he felt as if he had made a huge mistake. The horror at finding another man inside the apartment was almost too much to bear. He nearly left, were it not for the guy's hasty departure and Lindsay's cool explanation. At first he was surprised to hear the guy introduce himself as Ron. Didn't Lindsay mention a Skip at the coffee shop? Now he wondered if Lindsay had numerous guys floating in and out of her life. If that were the case, he'd rather not be counted as one of many. He didn't need or want competition.

Hold on now. You don't know where any of these guys stand in her life. As Candy said, for all you know, Skip could be her big brother and the other man her cousin. You'd better find out what's cooking first before you begin leaping to judgment.

Despite all the uncertainty, Lindsay seemed eager to have him in, so he followed along with the game plan. He sat on the sofa, slowly eating his third slice of pizza, realizing he should say something as they watched the Sound Of Music. What was he doing here anyway? An act of desperation? An illustrative example to convince his sister he did get together with other women? Or a test to see if they had any future?

Jeff pushed the questions aside and turned his attention to the movie. He found his interest sparked at the setting of the movie during the invasion of Nazi Germany. With American history his specialty, he also held a fascination for the world wars. His grandfather had stormed the beaches of Normandy as a young man and lived to tell his remarkable story. When Jeff mentioned this fact to Lindsay, she focused her chocolate-colored eyes on him. For the first time, he dwelt on her attractiveness—flowing hair, high cheekbones tinted red, and large eyes. No wonder guys were marching in and out of her life. Yet the real question still remained: Did she care about any of them?

"I don't know very much about World War Two," she said, carrying dirty plates to the kitchen. "Of course, everyone has heard about Hitler and the terrible things he did to the Jewish people in the concentration camps."

Jeff wanted to expound on the details of the war, America's involvement and so on but remembered he was here to scout out Lindsay's interests. Instead, he asked her if she liked other musicals.

Lindsay settled back in an easy chair and mentioned a love for *Fiddler on the Roof* and *Oklahoma* and another favorite, *State Fair*. All at once, she laid her hand against the back of the chair with the palm extended. With her head tilted up she began to sing. " 'I'm as restless as a willow in a wind storm. I'm as jumpy as a puppet on a string. They say that I have spring fever, but it isn't even spring.' "

Jeff stared, mesmerized by her voice and the way she carried herself with such confidence and pizzazz. For the first time, he felt an overwhelming desire to kiss her lips with the sweet melody trickling from them. *What am I thinking?* He forced the sensation down deep where it belonged.

"State Fair is such a cute movie. The girl refuses to marry

some country bumpkin who wants to live in an ultra modern, pre-fab place decked out in linoleum. Then she meets a newspaper reporter at the fair, and they fall in love." Lindsay paused. Her face turned the color of a poinsettia. She began to cough as if the words choked her. "Anyway, it's a cute movie. The family's pet pig wins first prize at the fair."

Jeff picked up his glass of spring water and took a large swallow. The ice chilled him. So far, he was enjoying this evening immensely, even if it was centered on simplistic things like musicals. Why complicate life with woes and confusion? How he wished every day could be this pleasant.

Suddenly, Lindsay rose and turned off the television. "It's a long movie," she said, "and it's getting late. I still have to make a few calls to sponsors, and they hate it if I call too late." She picked up the plastic case for the video. "Oh, no. You rented this, didn't you? We didn't see it all, and it's due tomorrow."

"That's okay. Maybe some other time."

"I suppose I could make my sales calls tomorrow."

"No, you need to do your work. I have papers to grade anyway. Which reminds me. The fund-raiser has been going great so far. We've hit the goal of three thousand dollars, and we're still climbing. I'm going to give it until Wednesday. The students loved the cash cards."

Her face shone. "I'm glad to hear that, Jeff. I'll bet you're relieved."

"At least this part's over. When the merchandise comes in, I'll still need to collect the money."

"That should go fine. I'll guide you step by step."

"You already have." He took a step forward, only to watch Lindsay retreat in response. He backed off. *Steady. Don't jump ahead. One step at a time.* "I want to thank you for everything. You do a good job at fund-raising. I know I didn't come off as the optimist at the beginning of the program, but I'm glad it's working out."

Lindsay smiled. "So you think you'll make an impression on your fellow teachers after all is said and done?"

"Without a doubt. And I owe it all to you." He opened his mouth, wishing he could tell her how much he liked her and ask if they could get together again soon. Instead, he picked up the video and headed for the door. "Maybe I'll run into you sometime."

"As a matter of fact, I'll be there Thursday. I have another program to start with the art department. Don't worry though. It's with the sophomores. There shouldn't be any competition with your program."

"I wasn't worried. You know what you're doing." His fingers curled around the doorknob. He didn't want to leave this pleasant atmosphere that warmed his heart but turned the knob anyway and opened the door. A blast of cool autumn air greeted him, bringing with it the scent of fallen leaves. One leaf circled around before coming to rest at his feet. From the glowing bulb of the outside light he saw a maple leaf painted a vivid red. The color of love. *If only it were true.* "Good night, Lindsay."

" 'Bye, Jeff. And thanks."

The door shut firmly behind him. He walked slowly to his car, scuffing up freshly fallen leaves as he went. A sudden loneliness overcame him. Now he had only stacks of papers waiting to greet him when he arrived home.

Once inside his own place, he looked at the mound of white paper glowing like an apparition in the darkness. He knew what many papers contained—meaningless sentences filled with historical errors and grammatical mistakes. He should get on Mrs. Coates to teach her classes better writing skills. He flopped down, looked at the video in his hand and inserted the tape into the VCR. To his surprise, Lindsay had stopped the tape right at the scene where the hero and heroine of the story confess their love. He watched the characters in the soft moonlight, singing a love song to each other. Maybe he needed to be like the hero and wait for the heroine to return and find her future. Maybe he should wait for Lindsay to discover if her future included him, without trying to push and shove his way into her life. He already had an inkling she belonged in his.

◈

Jeff stared at the calendar book placed prominently on his desk, wishing it were Thursday. He met with the art teacher running the new fund-raising program and offered his assistance on that day if the teacher needed it. Inwardly, his real motive in helping was to be with Lindsay again. Every day since the pizza gathering he'd thought of her with her head turned upward, singing the song from the movie *State Fair*. He rented that film also and could see why a woman would like it, with a brother and sister who each find their true love in unexpected ways. It held nothing of historical significance that whetted his appetite, but he told himself that whatever interested Lindsay should also interest him.

The students filed in for another day of class in which he would begin a discussion of the Lewis and Clark expedition. To his surprise, he noticed Jewel and Troy sitting on opposite sides of the classroom. He had never seen them sit apart before and wondered what spawned the distance. Troy seemed to have his head in the clouds, gazing at times out the window to the sports fields beyond. Several physical education classes were taking advantage of the warm fall day to kick a soccer ball around. Jewel sat on the other side of the room, doodling in her notebook or chewing on an eraser tip. They seemed as far as east was to west. When Jeff posed a question to the class, hoping for Troy to throw up his hand or shout the answer, he remained quiet and distant.

When the bell sounded and the students began leaving, Jeff stopped Troy, who was about to scoot out the door. "Hey, what's up?"

"Nothing."

"Nothing? I find that a little hard to believe. I'm expecting my straight A student to know the answer to every question. You look as if you're on Mount Everest. Anything you want to talk about?"

"No." Troy began edging his way to the door.

"You sure? We've had some good talks in the past."

"Look—I really don't need you hanging on me, okay? I can take care of myself. And I'm not your straight A student. I'm just like everyone else."

"Of course you're an A student. You have a great mind. I can see you as a scholar or a history professor one day. I want you to keep going. I'm thinking of having an advanced placement history class next semester, and I'd like you to take it."

"I'm not going to be a history major, okay? I changed my mind. And look—I'm not your prized student or anything else. I gotta go, or I'll be late for my next class."

Jeff said no more. His throat closed over, watching the young man shuffle off. Troy must be feeling pressure from the other students and likely from one source. *Robbie.* Jeff shook his head. He remembered his time in high school when fellow students badgered him and called him The Worm. It affected him greatly, more than he knew. Maybe he should tell Troy about that time in his own life. He needed to get past it and look to the future. Jeff shook his head. He doubted Troy would listen to much of anything right now.

Jeff ran a hand through his hair, mulling over the situation, when he heard a soft voice like a gentle breeze. He jerked his head upright to find Lindsay entering the classroom. She looked amazing, outfitted in a navy blue dress. He would have stared more, were it not for the cloud of Troy marring his thoughts.

"Hey, I just wanted to thank you for the great time the other night," she said. "I'm here to do a pre-start with Mrs. Meyer, the art teacher." She paused. "Is everything okay? You don't look so good."

Jeff sat there, amazed by her perception. Lindsay was beginning to see right through him. "It's Troy. I think some of the students are pestering him for being the hotshot of the history class. He's starting to lay low. He won't answer questions in class or even talk to me."

Lindsay set her briefcase down on the floor and sat in a nearby desk. "Do you think Robbie's in on it?"

"More than likely. I don't know what to do. I can't let Troy slip away. All the gifts inside him will be lost. He'll never reach the potential God has for him."

"He won't reach it anyway, without God."

"That's true. I was making headway with him. But ever since the field trip to D.C., our relationship has soured." Jeff sensed his frustration building. "I thought it would be a great trip where the students could discover a real God in American history. Instead, they seem to be slipping further away."

"Jeff, don't read too much into it. Just remember it's up to the students to decide for themselves what they're going to do with the knowledge you give them. You can't keep them from sliding down the slippery slope if that's where they want to go. You can try to keep them from going astray by talking to them. You can pray for them. That's about it. God gives each of us a free will."

"I guess." He blew out a sigh of disappointment. "You know, at first I was hoping the money from the fund-raiser would get me where I need to go with my teaching career. Teaching is great, but there's so much more to it. What I really want to see is these young people change for the better. Money isn't going to do it. Maybe new programs won't either. It's working with them, taking time to listen, showing them that God loves them and cares about them."

"Maybe I could talk to Jewel again and find out what's happening among the trio," Lindsay suggested. "She and I hit it off pretty well the first time. Even if I have to eat at that greasy spoon again."

"Greasy spoon?"

"You know, the Hickory Diner. Mom always called it a greasy spoon. I went there not too long ago with Jewel. They pile your plate to the ceiling with the greasiest French fries you've ever seen."

"If you think it will help—talking to Jewel, that is. I'd like to know what's going on myself."

"I can do that." Lindsay rose to her feet.

Jeff watched the dress she wore caress her legs as she moved. He found himself jumping to his feet as well. "Hey, I need to do some scouting the weekend after next. Want to come along?"

She crinkled her nose in such a way that he nearly chuckled. She looked like a petulant child when a plate of brussels sprouts was placed before her nose. "Scouting? Like Boy Scouts?"

He allowed his pent-up anxiety to escape in a rumble of laughter. "No, no. Scouting as in searching out a historic site. Baltimore to be exact."

"Baltimore! That's a long way from here."

"Only about two and half hours, if the beltway traffic isn't too bad. We'll soon be starting the War of 1812 in class. I want to scout out Fort McHenry, learn a few things, get patriotic. It's where the original Star-Spangled Banner flew, you know, and where our national anthem was born."

She hesitated for a moment. "Okay. I went to Baltimore once when I was a kid. I guess I haven't been much of anywhere since I was a kid. And when you're a kid, you never remember where you've been."

"Great. And this time we're on our own. No students."

"Sounds good." The smile she gave before exiting the classroom carried him through the remainder of his afternoon classes and well into the evening. He envisioned her singing songs to him, with the navy blue dress sweeping her petite form. Maybe on the way to Baltimore, she would sing more songs from her favorite movies. The thought helped to ease the anxiety he felt over Troy.

ten

The overwhelming stench of fried food assaulted her nostrils while Lindsay sat in the booth, playing with a spoon inside a cup of coffee. Jewel was already fifteen minutes late. She wondered if it had been a mistake to get involved with the students like this. Yet seeing Jeff's disappointment over both Troy and Jewel, Lindsay knew she needed to do something. She didn't know why Jeff's reactions affected her so much. Perhaps she really was developing an affinity for him. Did this signal the start of something new in their relationship?

She nearly laughed when she considered their rocky beginnings and the looks of disapproval that had once radiated from those deep blue eyes of his. Now she found herself becoming even more involved with him, to the point of accepting a trip to Baltimore. How could this be—the innocent fund-raiser suddenly hooked up with the grouch of Western High? Only God could help arrange such an unlikely relationship. There was wisdom in allowing Him to find her the perfect husband and in the most imperfect of circumstances. At the outset, Ron seemed a fitting candidate. He was successful, rich, good-looking, and he wanted her, or at least she thought he did. But the night he came, asking for a date, she saw something different. He was not the match for her. She would rely on God's peace to guide her and not her mixed emotions.

At that moment the door to the diner opened, and several young people walked in. She saw the top of Jewel's curly head and then Robbie wearing a sleeveless shirt that displayed his bulging muscles. Terrific. Why did she have to bring him along?

"Hi," Jewel said rather shyly, slipping into the booth opposite Lindsay. Robbie took a seat on a nearby stool and ordered a soda.

"Does he have to be here?" Lindsay whispered.

"Why not? Robbie hasn't done anything wrong. In fact, I think he's been great—showing me how much Troy was trying to control me."

Lindsay shook her head in confusion. "I thought that's what you wanted. You were literally begging Troy to announce his undying love for you. That's why you wanted the Goofy phone."

"I used to think so." She shook her head at the waitress who came with plastic coated menus, stained with dried ketchup. "When Robbie told me how a lot of the students are mad that Mr. Wheeler is giving Troy better grades on his essays and tests, it got me thinking. Maybe it isn't such a good idea hanging around him. I mean, I work just as hard as he does. Why should he get special favors just because he likes history?"

Lindsay gaped at the accusation before glancing at Robbie's back. He slurped away on his soda while talking to a friend occupying a neighboring barstool. "Jewel, none of that is true. The only reason Jeff, that is, Mr. Wheeler, took Troy under his wing was because he saw a great potential in him. He cares about all his students."

"I don't know. He sure doesn't act like it. It's like Troy is the model student, and the rest of us are nothing."

Lindsay could see the war Jewel faced—loving a guy one moment, hating him the next. Her mother often said when she was young that teenagers were kids and adults mixed up in one body. Yet, as she stared at Jewel's innocent face, she only wanted to help her. How could she keep this young woman from making the biggest mistake of her life? Not that Lindsay wanted her going out with Troy instead. Rather she wanted Jewel to look beyond relationships to the One who created relationships in His own timing. She wanted to convince Jewel that she didn't have to search for acceptance in people but could find acceptance and importance with God.

"Hey, it's getting kind of hot in here. Wanna take a walk with me in the park?'

"I don't know."

Jewel cast a questioning glance at Robbie. The look grated on Lindsay's nerves. Now who was controlling whom? When Jewel announced she was going for a walk, Robbie shrugged, to Lindsay's amazement. She thanked God for the window of opportunity.

Lindsay and Jewel meandered out of the restaurant. Orange rays of sunlight gleamed behind the brick buildings that comprised Main Street. She used to know every inch of this place, but over the years the town had changed and the people with it. She thought of herself and Ron and how different they had become since they walked these sidewalks and drove the familiar streets.

They walked along until they came to the park. A sprinkling of fall leaves covered the grass. A small fountain, raised by the support of the townspeople, shot streams of water into the air. Lindsay prayed for the right words that might minister to the confused young woman.

"Jewel, do you recall how I shared about Ron the last time we talked?"

"Yeah."

"Well, he came to see me not too long ago."

"He did? Wow. What did you do? Did you go out?"

"He wanted me to go out. He tried twisting my finger every which way to make me go. Somehow, I knew it wasn't the right thing to do. He had ulterior motives. Selfishness for one thing."

Jewel cast her a look. "How did you know that?"

"I could sense it. He really didn't care about my feelings. He wanted to put on a show and hoped I would come along for the ride. I wouldn't play the game. I think you need to consider if others might be playing games, too, and at your expense."

"Yeah, like Troy."

"Actually I meant Brutus—uh, I mean Robbie. I warned you about a war that might happen, Jewel."

"If you mean Troy and Robbie, it isn't happening. Troy and I got into a huge fight. He won't speak to me anyway. So I don't see a problem about hanging out with Robbie. Like I said, we go way back."

"I know. Ron and I did too. Along the way, people change. Their attitudes change. Many would rather look out for number one—themselves. Jewel, I care about you. I don't want to see you hurt. And, believe me, you'll be hurt if you allow yourself to get too close to guys like Robbie who are only interested in themselves."

"I can't tell Robbie to leave. His mother and mine are practically best friends. We see each other all the time."

"There are ways to make your feelings known. I made mine known to Ron, and he heard the message loud and clear." *That is, with a little help from Jeff.* "I did it so I wouldn't be trapped by emotion and have my life ruined. I want to do great things one day. I don't want to be sidetracked by people who might hold me back."

Jewel said nothing for a while but played with a silver chain around her neck. Finally she said, "You know, I've been thinking about things. I've been thinking about that trip we took to D.C. and how all those people did some great things for our country. Someday I'd like to do great things too. I know it sounds weird. I guess I'm just trying to find my way through this."

"It's not weird at all. Deep down inside, we all want to do great things. We want people to notice us. To tell you the truth, I found real acceptance in life only when I found God. I don't have to go searching for people to like me. God loves me for who I am. He knows what's best for me. You remember seeing those people in the paintings inside the rotunda—like the Pilgrims and even Pocahontas, who was your age? They decided to trust God with their lives. They found their acceptance in Him, and when they did, God used them for great things. Now they are remembered right in our Capitol this very day."

"It's pretty sweet what they did. Like Troy said, though, that was so long ago."

"They may have lived in another era, but God is still God. He is the same yesterday, today and forever. The same God who helped them is the same God who lives today. All you have to do is put your trust in Him."

Just then, Lindsay heard a whistle. Robbie sauntered up with one of his burly friends in tow. Jewel immediately rose and smiled at him. Frustration mounted within Lindsay. Jewel had been on the verge of accepting the truth, only to have the flame snuffed out by Brutus himself. *Oh, God, if only we had a few more minutes.*

Jewel said nothing more to Lindsay but allowed Robbie to hook his arm around her and escort her down the sidewalk. Lindsay watched them leave with a heavy heart. So close and yet so far. *God, help Jewel make the right decisions in her life.*

❧

Lindsay had just finished mixing up a batch of brownies when the phone rang. At times, when she felt down, she would hunt in the cupboard for the ingredients to make the chocolate squares from scratch, just as her mother did long ago. To her, there was nothing more comforting than scooping up a creamy mound of brownie dough and letting it dribble off the spatula right onto her tongue. Inevitably, after the brownies were baked, she would end up putting them in a decorative tin left from a fund-raising sale and give them away to a teacher who needed a lift. Maybe Jeff would be the recipient of this batch. He could use some cheering up almost as much as she did.

Jeff's voice came over the phone. "How did it go with Jewel?"

"Okay, I guess." Her voice strained as she mixed the thick batter.

"You don't sound very good."

"I'm making brownies. Helps ward off stress."

"Really. I didn't know that. I thought watching musicals helped in that area."

"Sometimes." She rested the spoon inside the bowl and plopped down in a kitchen chair. "I don't know, Jeff. I was having a really good conversation with Jewel. I was able to share God with her. Then Robbie hunted her down and whisked her away before the words even had a chance to sink in. I'm so afraid everything I said will become seeds that get picked off by the birds."

"I know. It gets frustrating. Guess all we can do is trust God with the fruit."

"Right now Jewel seems convinced that Troy is the problem in her life. It's so strange. She used to think the world of him. She sat waiting by her phone, hoping he would announce his love. Now she's done a complete about-face. I guess she feels Robbie is fulfilling her expectations in life. It's sad when people put value solely in relationships and leave God out of the mix." She tackled the brownie batter again. "Did classes go any better today?"

"No one seemed interested in learning. Half of them were looking out the window, watching a physical education class. It's like spring fever has hit in October."

"Maybe we're trying too hard, Jeff. We want to make things work out, but we're trying in our own strength. We do what we can, then we have to leave it to God to do the rest, don't we?"

"Sounds like you're trying," he said with a chuckle.

She spread the batter into the pan. "I'm trying to understand why things don't work out. The words I shared with Jewel can be like rain, I suppose, watering where it's needed. And if Jewel lets other things or other people dry it up, then there's nothing I can do." She heard a pause in the conversation and imagined Jeff, with his blue eyes staring into space, mulling over what she had said. "Anyway, when is this trip you're planning to Baltimore?"

"A week from Saturday. You still game?"

"Of course. Gives me something to look forward to."

"Great. By the way, I didn't tell you this, but I saw the rest of the *Sound of Music*. You stopped it right at a good part."

"I'll bet the part where the German soldiers were ready to escort the Baron von Trapp to his place in the German Navy.

Just right for a history fan."

"Actually it was the part when Maria and the Baron confess their love in the moonlight."

A tremor shot through her. Was he trying to hint? He couldn't be. This was Jeff Wheeler, the toad that used to croak on his lily pad. But in recent days he seemed to have developed a princely air about him. She thought back to the grand staircase inside the Library of Congress. All at once she was a princess in a beautiful gown, climbing each step in high heels, her gloved hand carefully lifting the corner of her dress in regal fashion. And there on the landing, clothed in royal attire, stood Prince Jeffrey Wheeler. His hand would reach out to her. When their fingers touched, electricity would zip through her. His blue eyes that so captivated her from the moment they met would scan her from head to foot. He would then escort her into the great hall with long shelves containing volumes of history texts and perhaps a bouquet of roses on a center table to break up the monotony.

"Hello? Are you there?"

"Sorry. I was thinking, uh, about books. Anyway, I have to go. I want to put the brownies in the oven; then I have to make some calls."

"Okay. Talk to you later."

She discerned a bit of disappointment in his voice, or maybe it was her imagination. Sliding the brownies into the oven, she continued reminiscing about a fairy-tale wedding within the Library of Congress. She could see a huge orchestra strike up a patriotic tune. A procession would lead right through the halls of the building, and there she would be in the middle of it, clothed in a flowing white gown and veil that masked her face. Jeff would be waiting patiently beside the pastor of her church. The pastor's face would be all smiles, ready to induct her and Jeff into the bonds of matrimony. And above them, hanging on the wall, watching the festivities unfold, would be the signers of the Declaration of Independence in the famous painting by John Trumbull. Lindsay couldn't help but chuckle at the dream. She was glad no one but the Lord knew what circulated in her head, and He was most understanding.

Yet, as she went to her office, she wondered if her dream was that far-fetched. After all, Jeff was the one who brought up the love scene in the *Sound of Music.* His voice sounded wistful in the way he described it. Lindsay entered her office and checked the answering machine. Listening to the messages one by one, she recalled the old days with Jeff and the tense phone messages they once shared. Now everything seemed different. An attraction had begun to build between them. They seemed more like a team instead of adversaries, each of them plotting and planning how to deal with the Western High triangle, while confessing to each other their likes and dislikes. *Could it one day lead to marriage?*

Get a hold of yourself, Lindsay Thomas. He hasn't proposed, you know. Besides the fact, do you really want to marry a history teacher? Do you want intimate dinner conversations to be muddled in Civil War facts or the sinking of the Lusitania? There is so much more to life, and you've only just begun to see what it has in store.

Lindsay closed her eyes. *God, if my life is meant to include Jeff, then I'll trust You to bring it forth in Your time. You know what's best for me. I never thought in a million years it would be him; yet it's so like You to bring about the impossible.* She inhaled a deep breath. *Oh, God, help me get ready for whatever lies ahead.*

eleven

Jeff eagerly anticipated the day when he and Lindsay would be alone to marvel at history and each other. He marked off the days until Saturday when he would whisk her away to Baltimore. He promised not to go overboard with the historical aspects of the journey. He would do his time at Fort McHenry, observing the sights, then suggest they investigate the Inner Harbor with its shops and eateries, or take a lazy walk along the shore of the river.

At times he considered the scene in the *Sound of Music*, wondering what it would be like to propose to Lindsay and kiss her in the moonlight. He shuddered at the thought. Who would want to marry a roving historical textbook? And what did he know about her, after all? Very little, except that she had a heart for the Lord as he did, as well as a heart for the students.

The week leading up to the trip had been a rough one. The students were loud and inattentive. Troy skipped class for several days. Jewel scored a D on her exam. When she came to argue an answer on the test that Jeff had marked wrong, he could clearly see the hurt on her face. She then asked him outright if Troy had scored the only A in the class. Jeff calmly told her it was none of her business and that she would do better to consider her own work rather than concentrating on Troy's. She left in a huff, no doubt to find consolation with Robbie.

At times Jeff felt the dark eyes of Robbie burrowing into

his back like some power drill, especially when he was writing on the chalkboard or adjusting the television monitor for a movie presentation. Jeff refused to entertain the thought that Robbie or others might be out to get him. The mere notion brewed fear, especially after hearing the countless news stories of kids bringing guns to school to seek revenge on their teachers. Jeff monitored his surroundings closely, including his desk, car, and even his home where he installed safety locks as a precaution. He didn't want to be a casualty of some student's anger.

During these stressful times, he found consolation in long talks with Lindsay who listened with patience to his anxieties. She also had a rough week, with teachers lashing out at her over late shipments of orders or orders getting lost in the hustle and bustle of her company. Jeff liked to think they could use each other's shoulder to cry on. He would love one day to feel her tender cheek rest on his shoulder. He would do what he could to soothe her misery, if she would let him.

The night before the scheduled trip to Baltimore, Jeff decided to do something extra special for Lindsay. He went to a store and purchased a picnic basket, complete with plates, silverware and two crystal goblets. He then headed to a specialty shop and loaded the basket with all kinds of food, topped off by a thick fudge brownie smothered in frosting and a bottle of sparkling cider to drink in the goblets. They would have a picnic by the shores of the harbor with sea gulls flying overhead. The sound of water lapping against the shore would serenade the moment when they gazed into each other's eyes. A gentle breeze would carry the fragrance of love.

After the purchases, Jeff informed his sister of the plan. Candy was all for it, recommending he bring along a checkered tablecloth to spread on the grass and some pillows. The table-cloth was fine, but Jeff's face warmed at the thought of their lounging on pillows. He thanked her, drove to buy a tablecloth and returned with the package to top off the inventory. A quick scan of the basket's contents showed everything neat and orderly, ready for a feast in the great outdoors. Inside the fridge the cider chilled, along with the cheese, ham and fruit. They would have crackers, some good multi-grain bread and, of course, the brownie. He fingered the rim of one goblet and then the edging of a real plate, imagining their sitting in a grassy area near the water's edge. His hand would then reach for her, drawing her close, feeling the warmth of her breath fanning his cheek, their lips barely brushing. . . .

Jeff jumped. *Wow, I never thought I would care about anyone the way I care about Lindsay. God, please show me how to act around her. Don't let me scare her off by doing something foolish tomorrow. Help us have a good time.*

The next morning, Jeff awoke early to spruce up the inside of the car with a good vacuuming and a little interior polish. With that done and the picnic basket loaded in the back, he heaved a sigh and turned the key in the ignition. The engine sputtered and groaned as if unwilling to awaken for any drive, let alone an excursion to Baltimore. He tried again, only to find a puff of smoke coming from beneath the hood. He leapt out of the driver's seat and backed away from the car.

Robbie did it. I knew it. My worst fear has come true. He thought of the precious picnic basket and heroically grabbed it out of the back seat before dashing to the duplex. *Get a hold of yourself, Wheeler. It's not like he planted an explosive or something. Yeah, but that car was working perfectly fine yesterday. And it only has thirty thousand miles on it.*

Jeff allowed the engine to cool before raising the hood. To him, the engine of a car appeared as complicated as a person's thoughts and reactions. He sighed and went to the phone to inform Lindsay he would not be picking her up.

"What's wrong?"

"It's my car. It was working fine yesterday, but now it's smoking. I just hope it's not—" He stopped. Lindsay would think him crazy if he verbalized his thoughts—that Robbie or someone else had damaged his car out of spite. "I'll call a tow truck. Do you mind if we take your car?"

"Sure, no problem. I'll meet you at your house. I'll need directions."

Jeff supplied them before hanging up the phone. If this were any indication of what the day had to offer, perhaps he should cancel it altogether. The mere thought that Lindsay had to bail him out of a trip he'd been planning for two weeks irritated him. He sat in the living room, tapping the armrest of the chair, his pride wounded. This wasn't the way he had envisioned the trip.

When he heard the sound of her car in the driveway, he rose reluctantly to his feet to answer the doorbell. Lindsay wore a smile like a heroine on a rescue mission. He muttered a quick greeting and picked up the basket.

"Wow! What's that?" she exclaimed, pointing to the basket.

"Nothing much. Just lunch."

"What a beautiful picnic basket! Where did you get it?"

"A flea market," he said with a grin.

"You did not. You left the price tag on the handle. Fifty-five dollars! Mr. Wheeler, no wonder you need a fund-raising project. This basket must have been woven out of gold straw." She bowed. "Oh, great Rumpelstiltskin."

"Hey, you weren't supposed to see the tag."

He grabbed some scissors from a stand and snipped it off. The humorous moment eased his frustration. They headed out to her sleek white compact. Jeff threw one more mournful gaze in the direction of his car before walking to the passenger's side.

"Ahem."

He looked at her as she came to him with her arms folded.

"I give you wholehearted permission to drive my car. Besides I can't stand city driving."

"Are you sure?"

"Of course. I trust you."

"Thanks." His self-esteem restored, Jeff opened the passenger door for her. "After you, m'lady. I decided our topic of conversation on this trip would be eighteenth-century colonial customs, or perhaps you'd rather I relate the facts surrounding this Rumpelstiltskin?"

"Or how about the frog prince?" She laughed. "As a matter of fact, I plan to bore you with my fund-raising stories. That will surely put you to sleep."

"Not a wise suggestion, since I'm driving. Better make the conversation riveting. Perhaps you can share with me more about musicals, maybe even sing a song or two." He began whistling the theme from the *Sound of Music* as he went to the driver's side.

Soon they were heading out of town and toward the highway that would lead them to Baltimore. He conversed a little about his car, avoiding any speculation regarding the car's sudden ills. He didn't want to stir up rumors. He had no proof Robbie had done anything malicious, but the anxiety of it all still teased him.

"Penny for your thoughts."

"Better make it ten bucks," he said with a wink.

"Those are pretty expensive thoughts, mister."

"Yeah, just thinking. Overreacting most likely."

"About the car?"

He shrugged. "There's little I can do about that. It's just that everything seems different. Take Western High. The students seem disinterested, the teachers aloof. Maybe it's my imagination. I don't know what to think anymore. I've tried to give this teaching job everything I had, but I feel as if it's not working out."

"Jeff, don't give up. You're a caring person who loves what he does and wants the students to learn everything they can about this country we live in. That school should be thankful to have someone like you on staff. Whether they will admit it or not, they need you there. Just remember—if God is for you, no one can stand against you. As long as you're doing His work, you can't be a failure."

The words strengthened him at a time when he felt whittled away to nothing. Lindsay had a confidence about life that he lacked. He wondered if disappointment, persecution, anxiety, or any of the trials people suffered ever shook her.

He fell silent for a time, concentrating on the drive and the feel of the car under his command. He liked the way the sporty vehicle drove and the power it gave. In no time they were making their way around the Washington Beltway. Jeff gave this section of road his undivided attention. Cars whizzed in and out in brash moves that unnerved him. His hands began to hurt from clenching the steering wheel.

Lindsay stayed quiet during this time, no doubt sensing his apprehension. At last he finished the treacherous section of roadway and headed north toward Baltimore. He relaxed in his seat and glanced at Lindsay who appeared steadfast and sure, like the mast of a ship in the midst of a storm. "Doesn't anything upset you, Lindsay?" he asked suddenly.

She jerked around in her seat. Her brown eyes grew enormous.

"I mean, you seem so sure of yourself."

"Ha. Looks can be deceiving. My life isn't all peaches and primroses, you know. I have my trials in life like everyone else."

"Tell me about some of them," he urged. "I mean, you don't have to, but I'm just curious. I need to know I'm not the only one."

She chuckled. "I would, except you're completing a fund-raiser and I don't want to hurt the rest of the program."

"What does that have to do with it?"

"Most of my trials happen on the job. You aren't the only one who's come up against obstinate people. I've seen it many times—teachers who shout when orders don't come in or get messed up in-house, students who steal my prizes or pocket the money for themselves. Once a student stole my purse after I had finished an assembly. He wrote checks on my account and used my credit card. That was probably the toughest time for me emotionally and spiritually. It was so unjust. Here I was, the innocent victim, and the bank came after me for bounced checks. I was doing something good, helping teachers raise money, and an unruly student marches off with my handbag."

Jeff swallowed hard, realizing once again that he had underestimated her. "I guess you have had it rough. Maybe you've discovered the art of overcoming trials and tribulations. All I ever see in you is confidence and a happy face."

"Sometimes I feel I should handle things on my own, but I know it's not right. Jesus Himself knew what it was like to go against hateful and hurtful people. He understands. It put a whole new perspective on my Christianity when I discovered that God understands trials because He also suffered. And He doesn't want us to bear them alone by firing up our pride, claiming we don't need Him. I heard a famous preacher say one time that we must need God every single day of our lives."

Jeff sighed. Not only was Lindsay beautiful, but she was wise. He thought of her as a pure white dove, resting quietly on a branch, even as it swayed violently in the wind. *God, this is a great woman sitting here beside me. She's a prize. . .a jewel. Please don't let her slip away from me.*

He continued to marvel over Lindsay's characteristics as he drove through the city of Baltimore, toward the harbor and the edge of the Patapsco River. When they arrived at the fort, his focus on Lindsay was replaced by patriotism and awe. They waded through the sea of vehicles to the walkway that led to Fort McHenry, home of the Star-Spangled Banner.

The fort, in the shape of a star and surrounded by a moat, stood on the bank overlooking the waters that once brought in the enemy from the Atlantic Ocean. Jeff immediately found himself immersed in history. He imagined that fateful day so many years ago—of men hurrying to their posts to arm the cannon when British frigates were sighted on the far horizon. In the air, the huge Star-Spangled Banner, Old Glory, waved defiantly above the roar of mortars and the shriek of exploding rockets.

Inside the museum, Lindsay pointed out a display explaining the weapons of war. "So that's where the phrase 'and the rockets' red glare' comes from in the national anthem. The

British ships actually did fire off rockets, much like the bottle rockets people fire off on the Fourth of July, only a hundred times more powerful."

Jeff brought her over to a scale model of the fort. "And see this? Remember the part 'O'er the ramparts we watched, were so gallantly streaming'? The ramparts were part of the fort's construction. Above the men flew Old Glory. Can you just see the flag, like a stream of color in the wind? Major Armistead, the commander of the fort, said he wanted a flag so large the British would have no difficulty seeing it from a distance."

"But why? Wouldn't that send the enemy sailing right for them?"

Jeff smiled at her large, questioning eyes that sought knowledge, like so many of his students. He was eager to oblige. "Of course, but they were proud to be Americans. They wanted the enemy to know they would defend their country. It's the same patriotism we have seen in all our wars when the colors are brought out in battle. Men believed it was a great honor to be a flag bearer in the midst of battle. The flag is a symbol of unity, freedom, and a spirit that will never surrender."

He inhaled a sharp breath, allowing the words to infuse him with strength. Heroes like Major Armistead should not be lost in a history text but could be models of character and virtue for today. Bravery and courage could transcend time, giving a future generation the ability to endure whatever trials lay ahead. Jeff vowed at that moment to pursue the goals he believed God had given to him. He would teach history, share about God, and help others realize their dreams. He would stand strong and not waver, despite the obstacles thrust before him.

Inside the auditorium, he and Lindsay watched a movie

about the battle. At the end of the feature, the curtains at the right of the auditorium parted to reveal a wide bank of windows and the huge American flag flying high over the fort. A rousing rendition of the "Star-Spangled Banner" made his hair stand on end.

When they exited a door and walked along a path toward the stone fortress that once withstood a mighty assault, Lindsay's sweet voice serenaded them.

O say, can you see, by the dawn's early light,
What so proudly we hail'd at the twilight's last gleaming?
Whose broad stripes and bright stars, thro' the perilous
  fight,
O'er the ramparts we watch'd, were so gallantly streaming?
And the rockets' red glare, the bombs bursting in air,
Gave proof thro' the night that our flag was still there.
O say, does that star-spangled banner yet wave
O'er the land of the free and the home of the brave?

Lindsay paused in the walk. She cupped her eyes to survey the landscape and the waters that shimmered in the noonday sun. Moving forward to an earthen rampart from the parade grounds, she again paused before the placid waters that once brought the invading enemy. "Can you imagine how scared they must have felt?" she asked Jeff. "The rockets exploding, the bombs bursting the way Francis Scott Key wrote? Yet they stood their ground. They would not give up, no matter what."

"It's a sobering thought," he agreed. "It makes us seem weak when we give up so easily after facing small trials here and there."

Lindsay turned. The sunlight glinted in her dark brown

eyes. Her eyebrows narrowed in a look of determination. "We can't give up either, Jeff. We have to see this through with Troy, Jewel, and Robbie, and also with our work. I have to face irate teachers. You have to face your students. Even if there are people ready to set off emotional bombs, we have to stand our ground and not give up the fort."

The fire in her eyes ignited one in his heart. His arms came around her, his fingers feeling the power and yet femininity of her curved shoulders. He expected her to pull away, but she didn't. With the flag flying high and the walls of the fort framing them, he lowered his face and kissed her. Her lips were smoother and softer than he could have imagined. She returned the kiss, and he hoped she wanted him in her life as much as he wanted her in his.

twelve

Lindsay could not believe what was happening. Just a short time ago she and Jeff had been like two warring factions, each trying to outwit the other, with their own goals and interests in mind. Now they had come together, hoping to affect young lives and, in turn, affecting each other. The kiss they shared sealed something in her heart—a commitment of love Lindsay never dreamed would come her way so soon. Once long ago she entertained thoughts of marriage, but only of old Ron. In the company of a Christian man who loved the Lord as she did, it gave an added depth to the relationship she had never experienced before. Their relationship was not based on physical attraction. She did not kiss Jeff for his blue eyes, though they were mesmerizing at times. She felt God had drawn them together to serve some special purpose. Exactly what she wasn't sure. She would take it step by step.

All of this left her feeling a bit lightheaded. While walking up the stairs, she nearly keeled over, were it not for Jeff's protective arm steadying her. When he asked what was wrong, she only waved it away, too embarrassed to tell him he had swept her off her feet. Instead, she suggested they find a pleasant place to have their picnic.

They found a spot beneath the arms of a large oak tree that may have been around at the time of the original "Star-Spangled Banner." Lindsay watched in amazement when Jeff produced a checkered cloth to spread on the ground and began unloading the picnic basket. They enjoyed a bountiful lunch amid the beauty of God's creation. Since the kiss, they had said little to each other. Lindsay wondered if the encounter had left him tongue-tied as it did her. What thoughts circulated in his mind, hidden beneath the crown of sandy brown hair that reflected the autumn sunlight? Did he have the same feelings for her as she did for him? Did he kiss her because he wanted her in his future?

When Jeff produced the rich brownie cake he had purchased in a bakery, Lindsay couldn't help but laugh. "That looks absolutely delicious. Did you know I gave the brownies I made the other day to a starving teacher? Got me a contract for a fund-raiser, too, though that's not why I did it."

Jeff cut her a hearty wedge. "So why did you decide to go into fund-raising?"

"I was a geology major in college," Lindsay explained between each delectable mouthful, far better than anything she could have whipped up at home. "I learned some interesting things, but geology wasn't for me. Then I got involved in selling books to families during summer breaks. I traveled around the United States, met some fascinating people, and developed a love for sales. One thing led to another, and I wound up in the parent company that helps schools raise money."

Jeff eyed her in concern. "That can be dangerous, waltzing around the country by yourself, doing door-to-door sales. Who knows what kooks are lurking in the shadows?"

"I traveled with a group. We girls kind of hung out together. We had one family that insisted they feed us a full Sunday dinner, complete with roast beef, mashed potatoes, carrots, the works. After living off macaroni and cheese, it was a little rough on the system."

"Macaroni and cheese!" he echoed, rolling his eyes. "Reminds me of my starving college days. I lived off that boxed stuff while waiting for the folks to mail a check for food or when I could get home to raid the pantry."

"We did it so we didn't spend the money we earned in sales. Most of us were working to pay our college tuition. In fact, we had a contest in the company. The one who could live off the least mount of money per week won the Tightwad Award."

"Huh?"

"One guy lived on macaroni and cheese dinners every night. He spent ten dollars a week for food and lodging."

"That's impossible. You can't live off ten dollars a week for food and lodging unless you stay at Aunt Edna's."

"Somehow he managed to do it. He found people who gave him food. He must have given them that doggy-eyed, 'please help me—I'm starving' look when they opened the door. He did have sad eyes, come to think of it. He slept in church pews or college auditoriums. Sometimes at the frat houses on college campuses he offered to cook breakfast for the guys in exchange for lodging. He got free meals that way, too."

"That's insane."

Lindsay nodded in remembrance. "It was something else. We all had to watch our budgets. During the two months I spent one summer in Los Angeles, we found a restaurant that had just been opened by Spanish Americans. They ran a special: chili cheese omelets, two for one. Six of us would march in there. Three would buy, and we'd all split the cost. We did it for six weeks."

Jeff gulped. "Six weeks!"

"Can you imagine? They never changed the special, either. We found out later it was because they thought we loved their omelets. One time," Lindsay began laughing, "I tried cutting my fork through the omelet and found out the cook hadn't removed the cellophane wrapper on the cheese before cooking it. Guess we had them flustered after a while, coming in there week after week."

"You've led an interesting life. I can't imagine eating chili cheese omelets for six weeks straight. I thought I was doing poorly by microwaving frozen dinners most nights."

"Those were the good ol' days," she remarked. She remembered all too well being out in L.A. and wishing she could get together with Ron who lived several hundred miles to the north. Now, in reflection, she was glad she hadn't stayed in contact with him. Life would have turned out differently. For one thing, she wouldn't be eating a scrumptious fudge brownie with an intelligent and thoughtful man on a crisp, fall day in the most patriotic of settings.

"So what about you? Did you go to college? I'm assuming you did, since you're a high school teacher."

Jeff nodded. "Sure. Went to college and got my teaching degree. I can't say anything exciting happened. I had a fairly uneventful life. I worked odd jobs in the summer. Once I obtained a teacher's assistant position with a history professor who taught in a community college. When I found out how difficult certain college students could be, especially when it came to their grades, it opened my eyes. I suppose it readied me for the challenges I'm facing now."

"We should invite Troy and Jewel on some outing," Lindsay suggested. "Get them away from their friends and other influences and spend some time with them. I think it would do them good."

"I would do it in an instant, except I'm already painted as someone who dishes out favors. Many students are in open rebellion because of all the gossip. I have no intention of fueling the ruckus."

"Then we should plan to bring them all here," Lindsay

mused, observing the American flag fluttering in the breeze. "Patriotism can be infectious. If we can show them this place—get them to understand the dangers Americans faced and how they overcame the odds—maybe they will be determined to face the future and do something great for our nation and for themselves."

"Careful, Lindsay," Jeff said with a wink. "You're becoming a history buff. Once you contract the disease, it's for life."

She sighed, amazed by her own reaction to the historical sites she had seen these last few weeks. She would never have believed that visiting historical places would do something deep within her. She had always glossed over historical facts and figures in her youth, thinking they meant little to everyday life. Yet history had much to offer. The heroes and heroines of the past taught her that the challenges of life were not so great that they couldn't be overcome. "Jeff, this has been life-changing. I've learned so much. I take back everything I ever said about you."

"Uh-oh. Like what?"

"You remember, those awful things during the fund-raising presentation, like putting a mug shot of you on a T-shirt and telling everyone your favorite food is a can of Spam."

To her relief he chuckled at the memory. "I'm glad you used it to get the students' undivided attention. A few weeks ago they would have sold anything. Now I don't think they would even sell a gumdrop. I'm just glad the sale is over. The products will be here, and soon we'll have the money. Maybe once the money starts rolling in, they'll get excited and start learning again."

"Why didn't I think of this? Jeff, I can figure out your results right now." Lindsay opened her purse to locate her calculator. "You wanted to raise three thousand dollars, right?

How many products did you end up selling?"

"I think around fifteen hundred or so."

Lindsay punched in the numbers. "Jeff, you're looking at close to a five-thousand-dollar profit." She glanced up to see his blue eyes, like shiny marbles, ready to pop out of his head. He stood frozen, with a hunk of cheese in one hand and bread in the other.

"Are you serious? Wow, I don't believe it. Five thousand dollars! It's a miracle. Do you know what this means?" Jeff stuffed the cheese and bread back into the basket. He took up her hands and held them tight. "It means we can take the classes to places like this. Sure, three thousand will still go toward the junior prom. I'm going to see if the extra money can be earmarked for special events like field trips. This is great."

"Let the classes know how much they raised. And when the products arrive, make sure the students have the money back to you in a week. Be firm with them. If you end up with stragglers, then you could lose money."

"No problem. Wow, I feel great." His hands tugged her, gently leading her around in a circle. The harbor waters swirled before her eyes, replaced as quickly by a view of the fort and then the parking lot. Around and around they went, with their laughter echoing on the wind. When they stopped, Lindsay could barely walk from the dizziness that had overtaken her.

"Everything is spinning," she said with a giggle.

"All I see is the one who has changed my life, for the better. Come on—I want to show you a few sites in Baltimore."

She followed him back to the car, wondering what he had planned. They arrived in Baltimore's Inner Harbor to the screech of sea gulls and large glass buildings housing the shopping and eating establishments.

"I thought you might like to shop a little."

"Actually, I've always wanted to try one of those." She pointed to the pedal boats for rent. Jeff eagerly pounced on the idea. The two of them were soon pedaling away across the smooth waters of the harbor, serenaded by the sea gulls, the lapping of water against the boat, and the short toots of a horn from a faraway tugboat. Their feet moved in unison, propelling them around in a large circle from one end of the harbor to the other before arriving back at the launch site.

"I haven't had this much fun since I was a kid," Jeff confessed. He took up Lindsay's hand. Together, they investigated the many eateries inside the food pavilion. Still full from the gourmet lunch, Lindsay shook her head at his offer of food until they came to an ice cream stand. He ordered two small cones.

"A perfect ending to a perfect day," he said, handing her one. His hand shook slightly, leaving a small dot of ice cream on the tip of her nose.

"Jeff!"

He laughed and took up a napkin to wipe off the smear. Ignoring the people around them, he lowered his head and kissed her. As he did, his cone tipped sideways, sending the ice cream sailing to the ground with a splat.

"Jeff!" Lindsay said with a laugh. "Look what you did."

"That's okay."

"You can help me eat mine." Together they feasted on the sweet confection that tickled her throat with cold, while they headed back to the car. Lindsay sighed in contentment. If dreams could come true, this day definitely topped any she could have conceived. History, combined with a romantic picnic, topped off by the Inner Harbor. And Jeff was a unique person with a giving heart. In the short time they had spent together, Lindsay felt her feelings for him magnified. She could already envision them spending a lifetime together, scouting out every place of history, listening all day to his explanations, and sharing in fun such as this.

Lindsay also knew relationships were filled with not only good times, but trying times as well. For as long as she had been a Christian, she knew trials shaped one's character. She grimaced at the thought of another trial coming their way. Would it be the trial of Jewel and Troy? Or would it be something else totally unexpected, raising its ugly head and announcing itself in some unpredictable fashion?

"Okay, now a penny for your thoughts."

"You don't want to know," she blurted out. She saw his hands tense and lines of concern form around his mouth. "No, it's not what you think. I had a great time today. I know the good times can't last, though—that we have to get back to the nitty-gritty of life."

"I know. I have a dead car waiting for me and students who would rather play with their Play Stations than learn history. But I'm not going to think about that now. I want to think about today for as long as I can."

Lindsay agreed. When she returned home, she would have fund-raising starts to prepare for in the coming weeks, calls to make, and appointments to keep.

The trip came to an end when Jeff drove into his duplex and the empty space where his car once stood. "Guess the towing company picked it up," he noted. Lindsay got out of the seat to help take out the picnic basket. "You want to come in?" he asked.

Lindsay nearly jumped at the chance of spending more time with him, especially after today. In the twilight, with the warmth of his presence so very tangible, the temptation might be there to throw caution to the wind. Knowing how fresh her feelings were, she didn't want to risk the emotions overpowering God's desire for purity and trust.

She shook her head. "I'd better not. It's getting late."

To her relief he agreed. "Sure. Thanks for being an excellent scouting buddy. I'll look you up again if I need more help."

He cracked a smile that ignited one on her face. Smiling came easy for her now, with these newfound feelings circulating within. He took a step forward. Would he kiss her good night?

"Good night, Lindsay."

He turned away without giving her a kiss. Lindsay was not disappointed but found his gentlemanly way of parting an added revelation of his character. It was a perfect ending to a perfect day.

When she arrived home, however, her next-door neighbor came to meet her, holding a long white box in her arms.

"This came for you today. The deliveryman left it with me."

Lindsay thanked her and took the box. She fumbled with a nervous hand to open the door to her apartment. Once inside, she untied the large red ribbon and lifted the cover to reveal long-stemmed red roses in a blanket of white tissue paper. A handwritten card lay on top.

Sorry I made you so uncomfortable, Lindsay. I hope you will forgive me. Ron

"Oh, no!" She shook her head, trying to squelch the rising tide of bewilderment and discomfort. *Don't read into it. He's back in California anyway. It's just an apology.*

Deep down inside, she knew it was much more than that.

thirteen

"Mrs. Coates, we made five thousand dollars in the fund-raising sale," Jeff announced proudly to the small lady standing in the doorway of his classroom.

He was in an excellent mood today. Across the back wall, Jeff had strung up a huge American flag and, next to that, a poster of the words to the "Star-Spangled Banner." It made his heart tingle to read the words that had come forth in song from Lindsay's lips at Fort McHenry—the same lips he was fortunate enough to kiss. Since that day, their lives had taken a sharp turn. Jeff invited her out to dinner Friday night. The meal had been pleasant, filled with conversation concerning their trips, musicals that tickled Lindsay's fancy, and even their favorite foods. Through it all, he was learning more about her and enjoying every moment of the discovery.

A week after Baltimore, Jeff found the fund-raising order waiting for him in multiple boxes left by the janitor on duty. He had just finished stacking the boxes of merchandise in alphabetical order, with packing slips scattered across his desk, when Mrs. Coates came to inform him of the faculty meeting scheduled for the end of the week. He swelled with pride at the amount of goods the classes had sold, certain it would impress the elderly English teacher who was an outspoken critic at the faculty staff meetings. If the students delivered the products to the customers on time, he would hold five thousand dollars profit in his hand by the end of the week, right in time for the faculty meeting. And he would relish the victory like an Olympic athlete who had just won the gold medal.

"That's wonderful, Jeff," Mrs. Coates said. "The students worked very hard. I must say, I'm surprised how well it went. I suppose I underestimated the success of this project."

You and about two-thirds of the faculty in this place, Jeff thought. "I'm glad the program worked out. Lindsay—er, Miss Thomas—does a wonderful job. I think we should talk up the success of the junior class fund-raiser throughout the school. Maybe other classes will sign up to do their projects through her company."

"I'll spread the word." Mrs. Coates nodded and turned to proceed back to her classroom.

Jeff smiled at the thought of helping Lindsay. He looked forward to the reaction on her face when he told her of the additional fund-raising projects he hoped to secure by singing her praises. A merry tune teased his vocal chords at that moment—a song of triumph he wanted to shout down the halls of this school. The trip to Baltimore had been a cleansing balm in his soul. Jeff never felt more confident than he did right now, and he owed it all to Lindsay. Lindsay was his dream, his miracle. He wanted to fill her mailbox with cards and her front doorstep with flowers. He would do none of that, however, until he knew how she felt about him. He would hold back until the time was right.

Jeff grinned when the second period class marched in, their eyes widening when they saw the boxes stacked in front of the classroom. The students in his classes had warmed to him since he'd put the flag in the classroom. They stirred to life at the lessons about Fort McHenry in which he touted the bravery of men able to withstand the pounding of a British fleet. He played the national anthem for them, explaining how each part of the song illustrated what the author, Francis Scott Key, observed that fateful day back in 1814. The students responded favorably to the discussion. Troy even perked up and asked a question after class. The enthusiasm Jeff had experienced in Baltimore seemed to be rubbing off on the classes. Jewel and Robbie still remained aloof, but Jeff hoped things would get better, especially now with the success of the junior class fund-raising project.

"What's all this?" several students inquired, pointing at the boxes.

"Why, it's the tests I've been promising to spring on you," Jeff said with a wink, quoting a line from Lindsay's fund-raising presentation.

The students stared in bewilderment. They circled his desk and the boxes, pressing close, trying to determine what might be in them.

When he had their full attention, he said, "So you really want to know what's in them?"

"Of course!"

Jeff waved the students to their seats. "These boxes are your tickets to the junior prom. They contain the products you all sold several weeks back. Now we need to give out the merchandise and collect the money. In a minute I'll call out your names, and you can come and pick up your box. When you deliver the items, you are to receive the money for the exact amount of the purchase. Checks can be made out to the school. The money needs to be turned in no later than next Monday. Those who have earned prizes will get them after all the money is in and the products are accounted for. It's important you get the money in, guys, so you'll have what you need for the prom."

Jeff turned to the list and began calling out the names. Troy came and took his two boxes without a word. When Jeff called Jewel's name, she came forward to pick up four full boxes of products.

"I am also pleased to announce that Jewel sold the most items for this class period," Jeff said.

Jewel's eyes widened at this announcement, before dropping her head and smiling. She made two trips for the boxes and stacked them on her desk. Robbie sat nearby, his desk the only one absent of any boxes. "Didn't you sell anything?" Jeff overheard Jewel ask Robbie.

"No. I lost my brochure and all. Anyway I didn't have time."

Jewel flung back her hair in a huff. "Great. Then how do you expect to go to the junior prom if you haven't contributed?"

A flush filled his face. Others began staring at Robbie and muttering among themselves. Jeff glanced at the scene unfolding before him. Perhaps the classmates' disapproval for Robbie's lack of participation might be the best tonic in curing the young man.

After class, Jewel went up to Troy. The two began comparing the items they had sold to customers. Troy offered to help Jewel carry her boxes after school let out, which Jewel accepted with a smile. When they left, still talking to one another, Jeff could hardly wait to snatch up his cell phone and tell Lindsay the news.

"You did it," he announced.

"Did what?" Lindsay said in bewilderment. "I'm innocent. I didn't do anything."

"You are quite innocent and very beautiful, too." He wished he could give her a kiss to express the love flowing through him. "I'm talking about that fund-raising ability of yours. I received the order today. Everything's here. And Troy and Jewel are talking again. When Jewel found out that Robbie did absolutely nothing to help with the fund-raiser, she began setting her sights on Troy once more. Troy even offered to carry her boxes home."

"My only concern is, with this newfound interest, do you think Robbie could stir up more trouble?" Lindsay asked.

"I don't think he can. The students aren't happy with him for neglecting his responsibility as a member of the class. There's nothing like the dissatisfaction from a peer group to set a wandering student straight. I think this might be an opportunity for Robbie to come around. Maybe he will even open up to some help in his life."

"I hope so. We don't want them pitting themselves against each other. Maybe you should think about starting up that history club you talked about. Get the young people together, and maybe through it you can do some extra work with them."

"Lindsay, you're a wonder." A real history club, as he'd envisioned when he first walked into this school. Maybe it would lead to other things too. When he hung up the phone, he set to work drawing up plans for the club, what they would do, trips they could take, perhaps even forming a type of quiz bowl team that could compete on public television stations or in national competitions. The possibilities seemed endless.

A janitor began sweeping the halls when Jeff finished up a rough draft of the proposal to present at the faculty meeting Friday. Everything was finally falling into place. If only he had been more patient and waited on God to fit the pieces of this huge jigsaw puzzle together. God didn't require a helping hand. All He asked was for Jeff to walk by faith and not by sight.

Jeff went home that night to call his sister about his triumphs in love and life. For once he had good news to share. Candy was not her usual perky self, having just come out of an argument with her new boyfriend. Despite this, she seemed interested in hearing about the new things happening in his life. Jeff used the opportunity to share about his belief in God and how he prayed that God would help him.

"I didn't think God was much into the matchmaking role," she said. "I thought He only liked those fancy church buildings and gold-plated seats. The money in all that decoration could feed a small country."

"God isn't for or against gold-plated seats," Jeff told her. "I know for a fact, though, that He's for *us*. I've seen Him work out things in my life. I'm living proof."

"I wish things would work out in mine," she said with a sniff. "Everything is falling apart. You might as well know. Sam and I broke up. It was awful."

"Have you ever considered—has it crossed your mind to call Anson?" He expected her to shriek over the phone and tell him what a louse he was for bringing up the subject of her ex-husband.

Instead, there was silence. The reaction shocked him. Candy usually had an opinion about everything, especially about something as sensitive as this. Finally, her feeble voice answered, "Anson has a girlfriend."

"How do you know?"

"I'm sure he does. I think I heard it somewhere."

"You don't know that for a fact. Look—I'll give you back your own advice. Until you know what's going on, why don't you call? At least you can get a friendly discussion going."

"It's over between us. We haven't spoken in over a year. The last thing he sent me was a scrap of paper with an obscenity written on it."

"Why not try an innocent phone call? You never know."

Candy laughed. "Now look who's trying to fix everyone's problems. Little bro to the rescue. You suddenly have a lot of confidence, don't you? I guess your life is going well, and love is kind. Are you gonna marry that woman you were telling me about?"

The idea jarred him. While he did love Lindsay, he'd never considered proposing to her. He gazed around his place. Papers were strewn everywhere. History texts littered the floor. He couldn't imagine her moving into his apartment, wading through the history books, trying to hang clothes in a closet stuffed with all kinds of junk, sharing a bed that was covered by an orange-striped bedspread.

He grew warm then and sprang to his feet. "I—I don't know, Candy. We're not quite ready for that yet. I'm just getting to know her."

"Yeah, I know. I leapt at the chance and got burned on the way down." He heard the tapping of her fingernails. "Well, maybe I will call Anson. Scare that girlfriend of his right out of the house. I would love to see that." She chuckled.

When Jeff hung up, he again thought of Lindsay. Would she marry him if he asked her? What if she said no? He couldn't ask her, not yet. He had no money for a diamond ring. Besides the ring, there were wedding expenses, not to mention the honeymoon. And what about that new computer he was saving up for? *How can you compare a life with Lindsay to owning a dumb computer system? Isn't she worth it?* "Of course she is. The problem is, does she think I'm worth it?"

ᴥ

Lindsay could not escape the fact that something strange was going on in cyberspace. Every day she checked her messages on the computer, and every day she found E-mails from Ron waiting for her. At first she answered them with one or two sentence responses. He e-mailed even more, as if her answers were outright messages of interest. How he could interpret her mail in that way left her baffled. She even told him she went to Baltimore with the friend he had met on her doorstep a few weeks back. Ron responded with descriptions of the great spots he had been to in California, including the amusement areas in L.A. and the glitter of Hollywood. Lindsay had the distinct impression that as long as she answered his mail he held out hope for some kind of renewal of their relationship. She had to put a stop to it.

With shaky fingers Lindsay accessed her E-mail to find several messages waiting for her. The company had sent one about the new sales products coming out for the spring fund-raising campaign. A bulletin came from the reunion site where she had first registered to find out Ron's whereabouts—a move she regretted from day one. Finally, three E-mails were there from the man himself. Ron thanked her for her humorous E-mail. (She did not recall her last E-mail being at all humorous, especially when she stated in no uncertain terms that it would be better for them to stop writing.) His next message suggested they get together for the Christmas holidays. He would fly her to California for an all-expense paid vacation. Lindsay gaped in astonishment. In the last E-mail, he sent her a sample itinerary for the latter part of December.

Lindsay sat still in her seat, stunned by his audacity. *I don't believe this. Is he crazy? Why is he doing this?* She hit the reply button and wrote:

Why are you doing this? I've already said I think we should stop with these E-mails and go on with our lives. Even if you thought my E-mail was funny, I meant every word of it. Please—let's just leave on friendly terms.

She didn't even bother to check for errors but hit the mouse button. How she wished a dozen times over she had never opened the door that night and invited him in. Now the past was digging its way back into her life, infecting everything she was trying to do.

Worst of all, it was coming between her feelings for Jeff. At times she caught herself comparing Ron to Jeff. Ron was muscular and tall; Jeff shorter and small boned. Ron had money. Jeff had little. Ron wanted to fly her out to California. Jeff thought it was a big deal just driving to Baltimore for a picnic under an old oak tree. "I have to stop this," Lindsay scolded herself. "It isn't right, and it isn't fair."

The phone rang. Lindsay prayed it wasn't Ron.

"Hi, Lindsay. I was wondering if you wanted to see a video tonight? I rented State Fair—your favorite."

Jeff! *What would he think if he knew I was entertaining notes from an old boyfriend on the West Coast?* She began deleting all of Ron's E-mails from the inbox, wondering why she hadn't done so in the first place.

"Unless, of course, you're as restless as—something or other in the wind. How did that song go?"

"I don't remember, Jeff."

"What's the matter? Did a client chew you out today?"

"No, it's—" Her gaze returned to the computer screen and the E-mail folder once filled with Ron's messages. *I can't tell him what's bothering me.* She looked over at her brochures in disarray on the floor and on her desk. "This place is a disaster," she blurted out.

Laughter echoed in her ears. "Is that all? You should see my place. Look—it doesn't matter to me, so long as I can spend time with you."

Lindsay closed her eyes, wishing there were some way out of this mess. In an instant she found herself in the same situation as Jewel—smack dab in a love triangle, even though Jeff had no idea what was going on. The guilt overwhelmed her. It wasn't fair keeping secrets like this from him. Maybe it would be best to let him know what was happening and how she was trying to defend herself from Ron's advances. After all, if God had it in mind for them to marry one day, He would want them to start working out problems together.

"Jeff, I have a situation here I'm trying to solve. An old boyfriend keeps hounding me."

"Huh?"

"You remember that guy you ran into a few weeks back when you came here with the pizza and the movie? Well, he's been e-mailing me almost daily and won't leave me alone. I keep telling him to leave me alone, but he doesn't get the message."

Silence ensued before a soft response came over the line. "How long has this been going on?"

"Not that long. It really started up after I—" Lindsay paused. Her throat began to constrict. The words became muddled. "This was before you and I were kind of. . .well. . . before we got to know each other. I tried tracking Ron down and used the information on a find-a-lost-classmate Web site. Since then he hasn't stopped pestering me."

Silence.

A tremor shot through her. "I know it was a stupid thing to do. I should never have done it. I wish I could undo it all."

"Just tell him then," came his calm, nearly ice-cold response.

"I tried. Now he wants to fly me out to California and everything. What am I going to do?"

His voice turned edgy. "How should I know, Lindsay? I mean, if you went seeking him in the first place, he probably thinks it's open season. And you did invite him into your house."

"He came uninvited."

"You let him in the front door, right? Look—I don't need or want the competition right now. Maybe you and I should go our separate ways until this thing is sorted out."

"Jeff, it is sorted out!"

"Sure, and now your old boyfriend is giving you a free vacation in response. Next he'll probably deliver a new Lexus to your front doorstep. Yep, it's all sorted out. I have to go."

"Jeff, wait—" The dial tone buzzed in her ear. *Oh, no!* She squeezed her eyes, trying to stifle the flow of tears. *Why is this happening?*

fourteen

Jeff wandered around in a daze after hearing Lindsay's confession. Although she seemed sincere in wanting to get rid of this Ron, the mere idea they remained in contact, coupled with the offer to fly her out to California, knotted his insides into a ball. How could he compete with some rich dude like that?

In the meantime, his concentration suffered. When students posed questions to him in class, he struggled with the answers. The money they brought in for the sales, he jammed carelessly in an envelope in his desk drawer. He had been careful in the past to deposit the money he received each day at the front office but now threw caution out the window. Inwardly he burned with embarrassment at the way he had fallen for Lindsay like some lovesick schoolboy. He told himself he should find out if there was really anything between her and this guy or if she intended to get rid of him. But he fought against the nagging sensation to seek her out and talk it through. Maybe his love for Lindsay wasn't as strong as he thought.

Lindsay called soon after their discussion and left a message on his answering machine, telling him how sorry she was. He listened to the message several times, hearing the plea in her sweet voice that stirred up the feelings he still had for her. They were quickly subdued with visions of the tanned and muscular Prince Charming he had met on the doorstep of Lindsay's apartment. The thought of competition by a surfer from California—sporting expensive clothes, a huge smile and a fat wallet—proved too much to bear.

One afternoon on his way out of school, Jeff met Troy at the end of the hall. The young man greeted him for the first time since the trip to Washington, D.C. Jeff nodded curtly before telling him he had a ton of work to do.

"I just wanted to say. . .well, I'm sorry for talking to you the way I did a few weeks back."

Jeff stared in disbelief.

"I guess I was mad that everyone kept saying you were showing me favors and all."

"I appreciate your telling me this, Troy."

"Anyway a couple of us were talking. We want to get together with some of the other kids and start planning the junior prom. We gotta book the band real soon. So we need to know how much money we raised."

"It should be close to five thousand. Which reminds me, I should get that envelope to the front office and not leave it in the drawer. It has a lot of cash in it."

"Five thousand? Woowee. That's more than—I'll have to tell him—them, that is."

"You'll have the three thousand for the prom expenses. The rest is slated for other class activities. Let me figure it all out, and I'll get back to you, okay?"

"Okay, sure. Hey—if you're still planning to set up that advanced history class next semester, I'd like to take it." Troy lifted his notebook in a gesture of farewell before taking off. Jeff watched the young man leave. God appeared to be in the work of restoration and just in time. Maybe it gave him a shred of confidence to deal with Lindsay and the big shot out in California.

Jeff strode out to his car in the faculty parking lot, glad to have the vehicle operational again. He had just opened the door when another car zoomed in beside his. A young woman peered at him through a set of dark sunglasses. She pushed them up on her head to reveal the beautiful eyes that still stirred his heart.

"Hi, Jeff."

"Lindsay."

"Can we talk? I'm used to having in-depth conversations at the Hickory Diner."

"I'm not sure."

"The only reason I even told you about Ron is because I didn't want any secrets between us." She pulled the sunglasses back down onto the bridge of her nose. "Please, can we talk?"

Jeff acquiesced, partly because of the encouraging conversation with Troy, but mostly because he couldn't resist the allure of Lindsay in those sunglasses. He followed her in his car and parked opposite the Hickory Diner. Inside the restaurant, they occupied a booth in the corner. The aroma of fried onions and greasy hamburgers filled the air. They each ordered coffee. Jeff dumped packet after packet of sugar and containers of cream in his coffee, not bothering to keep count. When he took a sip of the lukewarm liquid, he wriggled his nose.

Lindsay giggled. "You really are preoccupied, aren't you?"

"It's been a little tough recently. Here I wanted to watch a movie with you; then I find out Prince Charming is wooing you with free flights to the West Coast. It's a little hard to compete with that."

"Jeff, I tried to tell you on the phone that I want no part of this guy. I thought you understood. I wish I had the chance to explain it more."

Jeff sipped the coffee, despite the overly sweet taste. It gave him something else to concentrate on besides Lindsay's distraught face. "It seems to me you're keeping the door open."

Lindsay leaned across the table. The aroma of her perfume awakened him more than a full pot of coffee. "Jeff, I've made up my mind. If Ron thinks I'm leading him on, that's his problem. He has to deal with it. I'll be honest, though. Before I got to know you, I did decide to find out if Ron and I still had sparks left from long ago. Once I spent time with you and found out what a fascinating person you are, I didn't need or want Ron."

"I wish I could believe it," he said. "I still can't get over the idea of that guy standing there in your apartment."

"Jeff, I didn't ask him to come to my apartment that night. He showed up. I couldn't very well leave him on my doorstep. And the truth is, I'm glad you came when you did. I kept watching the clock, hoping you would rescue me."

Jeff's gaze lifted to meet hers. Rescue Lindsay from the prince of California? Could this be for real? He tried to discern her sincerity. Her brown eyes never wavered but stared directly at him. Her cheeks remained smooth, without a hint of muscular tension. She tipped her head to one side as if waiting for him to respond. "If all this is true, then why is he asking you to travel to California?"

"I don't know why. Look—to prove I don't want any further association with him, I got myself a new e-mail address. I also plan to change my home phone number. Most of my sponsors call on my cell phone anyway. Maybe it will convince you I'm serious about dumping Ron."

"You don't have to go through all that. Okay, I guess I'm a bit insecure. Maybe even jealous. I've never had a girlfriend in my entire life. When the right one comes along, I want it to be for keeps. I don't want to deal with the pain of broken relationships. I've seen it with my sister. I'll admit you seemed like the perfect one, Lindsay. Almost too good to be true. That's probably why I lost faith when I heard about Ron."

The warmth of her hand on his arm sent shivers racing up his spine. "Jeff, you're a great guy—fun, interesting, and you have eyes to die for."

He felt the heat fill his cheeks. Eyes to die for?

"By the way I can't wait to see State Fair. Any chance we can rent it tonight?"

"I suppose, if you have nothing better to do." He regretted the statement after the piercing look she gave him.

Jeff dropped some money on the table for the coffee and walked with her down the sidewalk to a small video store on the corner. He thought of holding her hand but kept his hands buried inside his jacket. Now, with everything laid to rest, he would go back to taking this relationship step by step. He did pray the steps would soon quicken to an all-out run.

❧

The events of last evening carried Jeff into school on a gentle wind of joy rather than a thundercloud of depression. Lindsay had popped popcorn, and together they sat on the sofa with the bowl between them, watching State Fair. Even during the romantic parts, when Jeff sensed a rising urge to take Lindsay in his arms and kiss her, he held back. He wanted to renew their relationship and bring it back to where it had been before all the confessions tumbled forth. Lindsay seemed to enjoy the evening very much. When she told him good night on the front step of her apartment, her eyes shone, and her smile was radiant.

That morning several students bounded up to Jeff, ready to hand in their money from the sale. Jeff nodded at them, taking the money while rummaging around in the drawer for the manila envelope that held the checks and cash from the last several days. His hand patted around the inside of the drawer. "Just a minute," he told the students. He slid open the drawer. No manila envelope. A jolt of fear passed through him. He pulled out the length of the drawer and sorted through every folder. He then opened the other drawers and pawed through them. *Oh, God, help me. Where is the money envelope?*

Students began filing into the classroom for their history lesson. They sat in their seats, staring wide-eyed, while Jeff continued to ransack his desk. When at last he glanced up, he saw the students looking at him in confusion. "Uh. . .open up your textbooks to. . .to. . ." He shut his eyes for a brief moment. "Just read the next section." *Where could the money be?* He searched every drawer then began hunting around the classroom. The students' eyes followed his every move. Whispers abounded. Jeff came back and collapsed in his seat, running a hand through his hair.

"Is something wrong, Mr. Wheeler?" one of the students inquired.

"I just misplaced something."

"I hope it's not the money," another student said.

The whispers grew to a tumult. Jeff ignored them and once more shuffled through his desk. Perhaps he had inadvertently brought the envelope home in his briefcase. He went through the leather case but found no envelope. His home was bursting with paperwork he would have to search through. *Why is this happening to me? If only I had locked that drawer or, better yet, put the money in the front office as I was supposed to.*

I should've never left it here in the classroom.

The second period class came in, bringing Troy, Jewel and Robbie. Jeff attempted to teach them but found himself unable to concentrate. Jewel and Troy exchanged glances. Robbie shook his head and passed notes to fellow students. When class ended, several students came up to him, including the infamous triangle, to ask what was wrong.

"I can't find the class money I've been collecting the last few days. Have any of you seen it?" Jeff stared at Troy and Jewel. "You both wanted the money for a down payment on the band. Did you take it?"

"Of course not, Mr. Wheeler," Jewel said. She looked over at Troy. "We didn't take any money."

"Where did you have it last?" Robbie asked.

"In the drawer here." Jeff ran his hands through his hair. "This is a disaster. If I don't find that money—never mind. Go ahead to your next class." Jeff left immediately for the front office, hoping he had placed the envelope in the school safe as he had done previous times. He searched through it but found nothing other than the money he had placed there late last week. He then went back to his room to check the figures. His heart sank. Several hundred dollars were missing.

What am I going to do? Worry and fear weighed him down to the breaking point. He groped for his cell phone. He had to hear Lindsay's voice. Deep down inside he was grateful they had reconciled. He knew she would have the right words in this situation. Instead, an electronic voice mail answered. He left a message of anguish and hung up.

After school was over, Jeff immediately returned home and tore his house upside down, searching for the money. *What is everyone going to say? Will they think I stole it?* He whirled, staring into the small cracked mirror hanging above his bureau. His deep blue eyes that Lindsay admired now appeared dull and lifeless. His hair stood up like some wild man's. "What am I going to do? If I don't find it—" He leaned heavily against the bureau. Someone must have taken it, but who?

He sat down on the bed amid the sheets and blankets tossed about in a fury after rising for work that morning. He tried to decide what the next step should be. He would have to do something quickly. If word of this spread among the faculty, they would no more trust him with a piece of chalk than with anything important in the school. He might even lose his job. Jeff pressed his eyes shut, thanking God he had spent some time reading the Bible this morning. He needed God's presence more than ever.

The doorbell rang. He tensed before rising to his feet and venturing to the living room. He peered between the blinds. Lindsay stood there.

"Jeff, I know you're in there," her voice called. "Please open the door."

He did so, slowly, only to find her arms thrown about him. "I'm so sorry to hear about what happened. Have you found the money?"

"No." He stepped aside to allow her in. He didn't care that the place looked like a tornado had passed through. Papers were everywhere. Books lay scattered across the rug. Cabinets were wide open with contents spilled on the floor. The scene illustrated his circumstances at the moment. He pushed some papers off the sofa for her to sit down.

"Tell me what happened."

Jeff told her how yesterday he had counted out the money

and put it in the envelope. He didn't bother to confess that he had been daydreaming about their relationship at the time and that he had forgotten to deposit the money at the front office. "Usually I try to keep the drawer locked when I leave the classroom. I guess I didn't do it that day."

"Does anyone else know you were keeping money in the desk?"

"Well, the kids have seen me with the envelope, but I usually take care of it. The only one I specifically talked to about the money in the drawer was Troy." He paused. "Troy wouldn't have taken it."

"I hope not," Lindsay began.

"He was interested in getting together with Jewel and booking a band for the prom. I made a passing comment about the money. I wanted him to know how much we had raised." His hand pushed through strands of hair. "What am I going to do?"

"We'll just have to screen everyone and find out who stole it."

"Right. These kids aren't going to say anything. I started to see a great change in the classes after we came back from Baltimore. They were taking an interest in history and asking questions. They scored well on the quiz I gave. Even Troy was showing an interest in history again. Everyone was excited about the money they had raised. Now this." He folded his arms in frustration.

Lindsay lowered her face, staring at the carpet, with hair like rivers of molasses showering around her shoulders. To his surprise she said, "I'm sure I didn't help any, telling you about Ron and everything while all this was happening. I'm sorry. I wish I knew what to do. I've had some things stolen, as you know. I thought having my checks forged was the worst disaster in my life. At any rate you should report this to the school principal and the police. This is a robbery, you know."

"Yeah, and it will be my head in the noose when word of this leaks out. Don't you see, Lindsay? This could be the end of my teaching career. Everything I've worked so hard for is gone. And it's my fault." He shut his eyes in despair, hoping that when he opened them he would see the envelope sitting on the coffee table.

Instead, he found Lindsay beside him on the couch, her arm encircling him, imparting comfort that he cherished with every part of his being. "We'll get through this," she whispered. "Somehow we will."

fifteen

Lindsay could not get the predicament with Jeff out of her mind. She spent time in prayer, asking God for wisdom and, above all, clues as to what might have happened to the money. The close bond she had forged with Jeff made her all the more conscious of his pain. Days passed, and each day Jeff called to tell her no money had been found. Lindsay even called Jewel to try to discover some clues. Jewel told her she had no idea what might have happened. When Lindsay asked her about her friends, Jewel blatantly denied their involvement.

"I wonder if Jewel might know something," she said to Jeff on the phone that night, sipping on a cup of herbal tea in the hopes it might calm her.

"What do you mean?"

"I tried to find out if she'd heard any rumors, particularly from Troy or Robbie. Jewel was quick to deny it, a bit too quick in my opinion."

"Everyone's going to deny it. I'd call the police in a heart-beat if someone confessed."

"So you're pretty confident it was stolen then."

"What do you think?" His voice rose in agitation. "Do you think I embezzled it? Everyone else seems to think so."

The insinuation shocked her senses. "Of course not. Most likely some student saw where you kept the money and made off with it while you were preoccupied."

"I hope whoever did this is having a huge crisis right now,"

Jeff said through clenched teeth. "This thing has been following me like the plague. The department chair has called me careless and inept. He said I'd better find out what happened soon." He sighed. "I pray that I'm wrong."

"Wrong about what?"

"Wrong that it could be Troy. He's the only one I specifically talked to about the money. He would have no reason to steal it, would he?" Jeff seemed to wrestle with that very question.

"You'll have to keep your eyes and ears open to anything. And pray."

"I have prayed, and I'm still praying."

Lindsay had, too, though she didn't say it. She hung up the phone, feeling sorry for Jeff and sensing her own determination to find the perpetrator. But how does one go about tracking down the guilty party in a large school? It could be anyone attending Western High. She would need inside information somehow. Perhaps she could offer a reward.

Lindsay turned to the computer and set to work designing a poster. She put in huge letters: "Take back your school from criminals! REWARD for information leading to the return of the junior class prom money. Tips kept anonymous."

I hope this helps you, Jeff. There isn't much else I can do. Maybe it would encourage someone to come forward. Although the reward would not match the crime by any means, perhaps it would lead them to the perpetrator.

Lindsay arrived early at Western High to put up the posters on all the conspicuous bulletin boards around school. She had just placed one in the hallway when an older woman stopped to survey the poster over the rims of her glasses.

"A reward poster for what?"

"For information leading to the person or persons who

might have stolen the junior class money," Lindsay explained.

"The students will say anything to get the reward money, you know. They'll lead you on a wild goose chase."

"They'll only get the reward if they find the one who stole it. And it would be helpful if the teachers could also keep their eyes and ears open. We could use everyone's help."

"I have no interest in bailing out a teacher who had no business putting a large sum of cash in an unlocked drawer in the classroom. Plain foolishness." The teacher began moving down the hall.

Lindsay bristled. "And no one has the right to steal hard-earned money from a student function, even if the money was sitting out in broad daylight. It's a shame we can't trust our own teachers and students in a school. We must keep everything under lock and key, twenty-four hours a day."

The teacher turned. "Perhaps you don't realize it, but this is the real world."

"It's a pretty sad world if you ask me. There's something wrong when crimes like this are committed so easily. When is something going to be done?"

The teacher disappeared into a classroom, leaving Lindsay to stew over the exchange. How the teacher could hurl the blame on Jeff and forget the one who committed the crime burned her to the core. She stuffed the stapler and tape back into the bag and marched down the hall, only to find Jeff approaching her from the opposite direction.

"What are you doing here?" he asked, somewhat bewildered.

"Trying to catch a thief. I've put up posters."

"Huh?"

She took out one of the posters from her briefcase. "We can't let this juvenile delinquent get away with it, Jeff."

"Thanks, Lindsay, but you'd better take them down. The school won't like it one bit."

She sighed. "I guess you're right. I don't want to make things worse than they already are." She put the poster away. "I'm only trying to save your neck from the guillotine. You have a nice neck, too."

He stepped toward her, his blue eyes softening, his lips turned slightly upward. "You're something else. Why do you want to hang out with a guy like me who can't take care of money?"

"Jeff, you had a bad day. We all forget things. I've forgotten things. I'll wager no one in this school is perfect, even though some think they are. They shouldn't be throwing stones at you. But if they do, you have God on your side. And He's big enough to get us out of this slight crisis."

"A slight crisis, eh?" He laughed. "Lindsay, what would I do without you?" His arms began to encircle her.

Lindsay pushed him away slightly, aware of the students beginning to file into the building for morning classes. "Jeff, not here," she whispered fiercely.

"Later then. As it is, I've been doing some thinking. I know we didn't go to Fort McHenry for nothing. I want to get the victory in this. This is war. I may have been caught off guard by my stupidity, but I still plan to be in my fort with the American flag waving above me at the end of it all."

"It's the story of life, Jeff. The hero must win out in the end, with the sword in one hand and the shield in the other. Only then can the hero and heroine live happily ever after."

The smile on his face turned into a broad grin of delight before he picked up his briefcase and moved toward his classroom. She was glad to see his resolve. The heroes and heroines of the past had encouraged a new hero to go forth in his conquest for good. Warmth rushed through her at that moment, and more than just the warmth of attraction. She had a true bond with this man that no trial could break. They had been put together for a reason, and they would make it through this crisis.

When school let out later that afternoon, Lindsay placed herself strategically near the front door, keeping an eye out for Jewel. She prayed beforehand that Jewel wouldn't be surrounded by Troy or Robbie. A belief brewed in the back of her brain that Jewel might be willing to help her discover who had taken the money from Jeff's desk. Lindsay felt she had enough of a friendship with the teenager after the meetings at the diner to warrant this experiment. She hoped beyond hope that Jewel might be the ticket to exonerating Jeff.

Jewel finally emerged from the building, her curly hair flouncing around her shoulders. Lindsay smiled. Jewel walked alone, just as she had prayed. Lindsay moseyed on over, pretending to head for an appointment inside the building. "Hi, Jewel."

"Hey, Miss Thomas, what's up?"

"Not much. What's up with you?"

"I have a ton of work to do." Ringlets of hair partially hid her face as she gazed at the grass. "I have a vocab test tomorrow in Mrs. Coates's English class. If I don't pass it, I might flunk. I already failed her last two."

"Vocabulary wasn't my strong point, either. Some friends used to quiz me."

"I asked Troy to help me, but he says he's too busy with his own schoolwork. Robbie got a new job after school, helping out at a pizza place, or so he's been telling me. I probably won't be seeing much of him, either."

Lindsay's thoughts went into motion. Robbie can't be a suspect then if he's working. He would have no need of extra cash right now if he stole the money. Plus, teenagers aren't that eager to work when they could be hanging out with their friends.

"Are you okay?" Jewel asked.

"Oh, sure, just thinking." Lindsay accompanied her down the sidewalk. "So what's Troy up to these days?"

Jewel shrugged. "Who knows? He's been real quiet lately. When I try to catch him after school, he's already gone. I don't know, Miss Thomas, but I feel like I'm losing my friends."

"I'm sorry about that, Jewel."

"Then it got me thinking and all about what you said— how I shouldn't be looking for relationships with guys, just to feel wanted. Robbie told me I shouldn't listen to you. He said you and Mr. Wheeler are religious types with weird ideas."

"Everything I told you is true, Jewel. And it's not because I want to jam my religion down your throat. It's because I care about you and I don't want to see you hurt. Broken relationships can be some of the toughest times we go through in life. It hurts us right in the heart where it counts. And it's hard to get over. That's why I made a commitment to God long ago to let Him run my life. I told Him, 'Hey, You made me. You know me inside out. You know who's the best guy for me.'"

"Like Mr. Wheeler?" She cracked a smile.

Lindsay's mouth fell open.

"Oh, we talk about it all the time—how you two went on this romantic trip to Baltimore. We know you've been going around the school today, trying to find out who stole the class money. In fact, there are a couple of kids betting on when you two will walk down the aisle."

Lindsay gasped. The mere idea sent chills racing through her. "That's nonsense," she blurted out, though she didn't mean it. Many times Lindsay wondered if she and Jeff were destined to tie the knot. Hardly a day went by that she did not fantasize about ascending a grand staircase in a gown fit for a queen, ready to meet her bridegroom.

To her surprise Jewel elbowed her. "C'mon—you can tell me. I'll keep it quiet."

"I can tell you that Jeff—that is, Mr. Wheeler—and I are good friends." She hooked her arm through Jewel's, ushering her down the sidewalk. "If you want to know the honest truth—and please keep this between us—I think Mr. Wheeler and I might have a future together."

Jewel giggled. "I knew it. When you all came back from Baltimore, Mr. Wheeler had this weird look on his face. He bumped into his desk once or twice. In the middle of a lecture he forgot what he was talking about. It doesn't surprise me a bit he lost the money. He hasn't been thinking right at all lately. I knew right away what it was. L-O-V-E."

Just the notion Jeff might have lost the money over her sent another round of shivers racing through Lindsay. She steadied her shaking hands. "Anyway, have you heard anything through the grapevine in school as to who might've taken the money? You all earned it, you know. I'd think you'd want to know who stole it, rather than seeing your hard work go to waste."

Jewel became quiet for a moment before her soft voice responded. "I've just heard rumors. There's no proof."

"Sometimes what one person says can go a long way," Lindsay coaxed, eager for any hint that might resolve this situation and restore Jeff's reputation.

Jewel continued her silence.

Lindsay decided not to press the issue. When they strode up to a park bench, she suggested quizzing Jewel on the vocabulary for the upcoming test. Jewel pounced on the offer with glee. They sat opposite each other while Lindsay read off the list of words from the notebook inside Jewel's backpack. When Jewel missed a word, Lindsay told her to repeat the definition then use it in a sentence.

"You should have been a teacher," Jewel said with a laugh. "You sure know what you're doing."

"I had to learn the hard way, like most people. Life isn't easy, Jewel. We all learn difficult lessons, but they help us become better people in the end. And I have a good feeling at the end of all this that you're going to be a great business-woman. You won't be swayed by pressure but will do the right thing, no matter what happens."

Jewel lowered her head and ran a finger across the painted boards of the bench. "Ouch!" she complained as a huge splinter punctured her fragile skin.

"Let me see." Lindsay took hold of Jewel's finger and saw the edge of the splinter jutting out. She rummaged in her handbag for a small Swiss army knife and, in the collection of tiny tools, pulled out a pair of tweezers.

"I'm prepared for these kinds of emergencies," she said with a smile, taking hold of Jewel's finger. With the tweezers she gently removed the splinter.

"Wow! You did that quick," Jewel marveled. "I should get one of those knife thingies. They don't allow them on school property, though."

"It's my all-in-one tool kit. Screwdriver, tweezers, nail file, saw—what I would use a saw for, who knows—and a toothpick."

She gazed at her wounded finger. "Thanks so much, Miss Thomas. Between this and helping me with my vocabulary, it's been real sweet."

"I want you to know that people care, Jewel. And, as I said, you're special. Don't forget it."

Jewel slung her backpack over one shoulder. "I'd better get going. Thanks again for everything."

"Sure." Lindsay slipped her a business card. "If you ever need to talk sometime, call me on my cell."

Jewel gazed at Lindsay with moss green eyes; her lips parted as if she dearly wanted to share with Lindsay all the things she kept buried within. Lindsay could see the walls beginning to crumble and a bridge of trust taking its place. Jewel tightened her hand around the card, nodded her head, and shuffled off down the sidewalk.

Lindsay sighed as she tucked the tool back in her purse. She had come close to learning who may have taken the money. Jewel more than likely held an important clue. If only the bridge of trust were complete, then perhaps Jewel would feel comfortable confiding in her. Lindsay feared time would run out before that could be accomplished.

Lindsay had nearly arrived home when her cell phone rang. It was Jewel. "Miss Thomas, I wanted you to know—I didn't think it could be true which is why I didn't say anything at the park, but you've been so nice to me. I need to talk to someone. Anyway, I don't know if this is true or not, but everyone says Troy took the money. He wanted to prove to everyone he could do it and that he wasn't teacher's pet."

Lindsay tried hard not to choke at this confession. She succeeded in stifling it into a few light coughs. "Are you sure, Jewel?"

"It's just what the kids are saying. I guess the only way to find out is to ask Troy. I mean, it could be the reason he's been acting so weird lately. You know, when we all got our stuff for the fund-raising project, he seemed better. He helped me carry my stuff home and everything. Now he's distant again. I don't know if it's family problems or because of the money."

"I know this was a hard thing to do, Jewel, but thank you so much." Lindsay conversed a bit longer, reassuring the young woman she had done the right thing. Lindsay then inhaled a deep breath before punching in Jeff's number, knowing he would not be pleased to hear this news.

sixteen

"I didn't steal anything!"

Troy's reddening ears and quivering lower lip met Jeff's gaze. He had just stopped by Troy's house and found the young man riding what appeared to be a new bicycle. When Lindsay first related the news she'd heard from Jewel, Jeff could hardly believe it. Even though it had been rough going for a while, he and Troy seemed to be on better terms, until the money disappeared. In the weeks following the incident he had seen Troy turn into an introvert once again. Could this be a sign of guilt, like the signs manifesting now in the young man's crimson ears and flushed face?

"Troy, it's better we deal with this now. I know it's hard."

"You don't know anything. You think you have all the answers 'cause you're a do-good Christian, but you don't know. You don't know what it's like to have others gang up on you." Troy mounted his bicycle.

"I know a lot more than you think. We don't have to be controlled by the bad things in this world, or bad people for that matter. You can be free from it. We've been learning about the cost of freedom in history. The founding fathers wanted a land free from tyrannical forces, but in order to get it, they had to trust in someone other than themselves."

Jeff paused to collect his thoughts. "You remember the time we studied about the American troops in New York City during the Revolutionary War and how the Continental

Army was trapped, with the enemy approaching? General Washington wrote out a general order in May 1776 proclaiming a day of fasting and prayer, asking for God's mercy on them. Not long after, God caused a thick fog to come over the whole area, enabling Washington and his army to escape Howe's forces. They would have been destroyed if they'd stayed there. Instead, they prayed and believed in God. They knew they must have God's help if they were to escape the enemy."

"What does that have to do with me?" His voice began to quiver.

"You have enemies, too, Troy. I know you do. I just want to know how you plan to handle it. What are you going to do?"

Troy's new bike clattered to the hard pavement. He plopped down on the ground and buried his head in his arms. "There wasn't any other way. Robbie said he would lay off and I could have Jewel if I did it. He said if I didn't do it, his friends would get me. They had already trashed my locker. He was telling lies about me all over school. He had Jewel wrapped around his finger, telling her lies too. I couldn't deal with all of them. What was I supposed to do?"

"So you took the money?"

"Robbie said he would give me a cut. I got a hundred out of it, and he took the rest. Bought that dumb bike—but I've felt sick about it ever since. I can't eat or anything."

"Is there anyway you can get Robbie to confess his role in this?"

Troy peered up at Jeff. "Why?"

"Because if word of this gets out, Robbie will put all the blame on you. We need to get a confession out of him also. But it won't let you off the hook. You and Robbie will have to face the consequences, which could mean disciplinary action, maybe even expulsion."

"You mean they could kick me out of school? Oh, man, I don't believe it." Troy rose to his feet with tears streaming down his face. He went and kicked the bicycle. "Man, I don't believe this. My life is ruined, Mr. Wheeler, and I can't do a thing about it. And it's not fair. I had to do it. They were going to get me."

"Life isn't fair."

Troy jerked his head around. "You don't know anything about it. You weren't there, seeing my dad drunk every day and watching him leave my mom. And now I've got this gang after me."

"It's true I don't know everything. But I do know Someone who had it a lot worse."

"Yeah, I'll bet."

"He had everything go wrong. He was only trying to help others, but people were jealous of him. They spit on him and called him names. He even had a knife thrust into his side by a gang of thugs. Finally, they killed him right out in public."

Troy stared wide-eyed. "Who was that?"

"I'm talking about the Man Himself. Jesus. That's exactly what happened to Him. He only wanted to help others, yet He was stripped down to nothing, nailed on a cross, and put on display for everyone to gawk at. Jesus suffered abuse big time—but He decided to do something about it. He wanted something good to come out of something bad."

Jeff saw it in Troy's eyes—the disbelief, as if he had never heard such a vivid example of Christianity.

The young man began to stammer. "Y—yeah. B—but that was a long time ago. It doesn't mean anything now."

"It means even more now, because we are the ones He died for. Jesus died so even if we do things wrong, we can come out with a clean slate. We can get rid of all that junk in our lives. We can have peace, even if there are enemies after us. Jesus went through all the abuse and ridicule so that you and I can have a better life with God in the middle of it. And I'll tell you, God is great at getting people out of their worst messes. Ask George Washington—or me for that matter." He smiled inwardly, knowing how much he needed God to heal his own messes in life.

"Not mine," Troy's voice spoke softly. "I'm in too deep. I can't get out of it."

Jeff came and sat down in the grass beside him. "How about talking to God about it? He's a good listener."

Troy nodded. Together with Jeff, he confessed his wrongs and the pain he carried. When they finished, Troy looked at him. "Now what should I do?"

"We'll have to inform the principal what happened, then we'll see how this all plays out. You'll have to take whatever punishment they give you, but at least you won't have your conscience bothering you anymore. Most important, you have God on your side." Jeff hurried to his car and took out a Bible he kept inside. "Here. Take this with you. There's some good reading in there about warfare. Read Ephesians, chapter six. It talks about getting your armor on for war. And read the Gospel of John, too. It will tell you all about Jesus and what He did."

"I still don't know what's going to happen to me."

"We'll take it one step at a time."

❧

Not long after Jeff talked to Troy, Robbie was arrested for

trying to cash a check from the fund-raising sale at a nearby bank. Both Troy and Robbie were summoned to a meeting of the school board who elected to suspend them and ordered them to seek counseling and pay full restitution.

Though the junior class had the money for the prom preparations, the school elected not to give Jeff the extra funds for the history club but to use it for other resources. "I guess it isn't the right time," he said glumly while on an afternoon walk with Lindsay. The trees, highlighted in red and golden leaves, waved their colorful branches. Cows mooed from a distant field. Before them, the Blue Ridge Mountains rose up to greet them in colorful splendor.

"Things never turn out the way we expect," Lindsay agreed. "But you can't give up hope that it may come to pass one day. At least we discovered who took the money. Have you spoken to Troy since the incident?"

"I saw him a few times during his suspension to bring over some history lessons. He wasn't very happy. I kept reminding him that God was with him and this will pass. He can look forward to a bright future. I'm thinking of maybe taking him to a youth rally that's coming up in a few weeks. There will be some speakers and music by Christian rock bands. Maybe even Robbie will come along. That would be interesting, wouldn't it?"

Lindsay cast him a look. "A youth rally? You're stepping out of your playing field, Mr. Wheeler. What happened to strolls in Civil War battlefields or touring a history museum?"

"Those things are important, too, but I still believe God wants us to reach out to these students. And I want them to trust me, even after what's happened. I want them to know I forgive them, though my life was pretty miserable for a couple of days."

"Oh, these faith-building times," Lindsay said with a smile. "Harder than a full work-out in a gym."

"It can be painful. When you come out of it, though, you feel stronger." He paused, rolled up the sleeve of his Rugby shirt and performed a few muscle-building maneuvers. "So what do you think?"

Lindsay took hold of some skin on his lower arm and tugged. "Boing."

"Hey!"

"Just kidding. I know you're no weakling, especially after all this. I do believe you have held down all of Fort McHenry on your own."

Jeff then broke into a song from a musical they'd rented last week. " 'Oh, what a beautiful morning! Oh, what a beautiful day! I've got a beautiful feeling; everything's going my way.' "

Lindsay jumped in. " 'I'm gonna wash that man right outta my hair. I'm gonna wash that man right outta my hair. I'm gonna wash that man right outta my hair, and send him on his way.' "

Jeff whirled. "What kind of song is that?"

"It's from the musical South Pacific. You haven't seen it yet."

"I'm not sure I will. I don't think I'd like it."

"You would." She hooked an arm through his. The gesture sent warmth flowing through him. "It has a happy ending."

He paused to gather her in his arms, beside a wide-open meadow where grasses waved in the breeze. "Like this?" When he kissed her, sparks flew. He knew this was the woman he wanted to marry. Dare he propose to her here in this wonderful country setting? It seemed so right and yet so ill timed. He had no money like that guy out in California. He couldn't ask her to marry a pauper, and she would have to earn the bread and butter right along with him. He disengaged from the embrace, took up her hand, and strolled on.

"What's the matter?" she asked.

"Just thinking about the future. Lindsay, I—" He paused. The words became bottled up in his throat. He couldn't tell her what was going on inside him, not until he knew their future was secure. He swallowed down his response. "I really enjoy being with you."

"That makes two of us. I don't know any guy who would sit around watching musicals and even learning the words to the songs. You're unique, Jeff Wheeler."

When they parted that evening, Jeff had to wonder what it meant to be unique and if one could base a relationship on that. He returned home to find the light blinking on his answering machine. It was an urgent message from Candy, asking that he call her right away. The distress in her voice made his heart bounce around like a fish out of water. As he punched in her phone number with a nervous finger, he hoped the advice he had given regarding her ex-husband, Anson, would not blow up in his face.

The phone rang endlessly until a breathless voice answered. "Oh, Jeff, you wouldn't believe it. You just wouldn't. I don't know what to do. You got me into this, and now I don't know what to do."

"Hold on, Candy. Slow down. What happened?"

"Anson asked me out. Can you believe it?" Jeff heard the closet door open and the shuffle of hangers. "I don't have a thing to wear. Can you believe he asked me out? My own ex? This is unreal."

"What happened to his girlfriend?"

"They had a fight about the same time Sam and I did. Pretty

coincidental, don't you think?" Silence came over the line for a moment. When her voice returned, it was soft and a bit curious. "Jeff, would this have anything to do with your God?"

"My God? He's your God, too. He's everyone's God."

"You know what I mean. You were telling me how you prayed to God to help you solve problems. Now look what's happened. Never in a million years would I have thought Anson would show interest in me." She broke down in tears. "I thought I was an old shoe in his eyes. That's why he left me for another woman. I thought—I thought I wasn't good enough in the—well, you know what I mean. I hear about guys who don't love their wives anymore 'cause they don't feel satisfied. I tried to do things right."

"Candy—"

"I did everything I thought I should do. Why is he coming back, Jeff? Maybe he's just tired of the old girlfriend now and thinks it's time for something new. I don't want us to fall in love again, only to have him walk out on me."

"Why don't you come and visit me?"

"Visit you? What's that got to do with Anson walking out on me?"

"I'm just saying, maybe Anson and I could talk about things. Get a family connection in the works. Might make it harder for him to leave."

"Jeff, you're not even married. What words of wisdom could you possibly offer?"

"I can tell you for a fact that the only way you two are going to have a future together is if you let God take control of it. That's the problem. We think we have a handle on everything. Only God holds the key to success in our lives. He knows the past, the present, and the future."

Once Jeff said these words, he realized his own lack of faith in not allowing God to take control of his relationship with Lindsay. He had allowed everything else to get in the way. While he still believed he needed financial security before he popped the big question, at least he ought to feel secure enough knowing God would keep him on the right track.

"So what do you think?" Candy asked.

"Huh?"

"I knew it. Typical male, never listening. Open your ears, little bro. How about Thanksgiving?"

"You mean you want to come here for Thanksgiving? Sure, that would be great! Then you can meet Lindsay. She's one of a kind."

"I have to get going. Anson's coming in an hour to pick me up. I haven't had a shower yet, and all my clothes are from the nineties. I have nothing new to wear."

"Candy, just be yourself and not someone else."

"Hey, you know what? You're an awesome brother."

Jeff smiled before hanging up the phone. He would tell Lindsay as soon as he could that no matter what happened, with God leading them, they would be there for each other through thick and thin, for better or for worse, until death do them part.

epilogue

"I can't believe I'm back here."

The grand hall appeared as majestic as she imagined—the mosaics, the carved buttresses and statues, the winding staircase. Her hand went to her heart. If only she were clad in some glittering ball gown, wearing long gloves to her elbows, with pearls wrapped around her neck and a tiara in her hair. On her feet would be glass slippers, though she would make certain they stayed put at midnight. Instead, she glanced down at her simple outfit of pleated trousers, red turtleneck, and blazer. She pushed the bag carrying her belongings up over her shoulder.

"Hey, Miss Thomas, Mr. Wheeler wants to see you," Jewel said, running up to meet her.

Lindsay smiled at the young, carefree woman who had a glow in her emerald eyes. Jewel had given her heart to the Lord at the youth revival meeting they'd recently attended. Lindsay and Jeff had taken several students to the revival and found many of them responsive to the gospel message. They rejoiced over the young people brought into the kingdom of God. Robbie, though, refused to go and eventually dropped out of school, much to their disappointment.

Lindsay now gazed again at the beautiful architectural displays within the Library of Congress before turning to the staircase. She climbed the steps one by one, until a vision caught her in midstride. Her breath left her for a moment.

Jeff stood on the landing, holding what appeared to be a flower in his hand. "M'lady," he said with a bow, giving her a long-stemmed, red rose.

Jewel giggled and poked Troy in the ribs. "Isn't this romantic?"

Lindsay took the flower and something else that felt velvety soft. She opened the palm of her hand to see a small box. Tremors seized her at that moment. "Jeff," she began. Lindsay handed her rose to Jewel and opened the box with nervous fingers. Inside was a small but beautiful diamond in a gold setting, glittering in the light of the great hall. Her dream had come true.

"This is what I like!" Troy hooted. "An engagement right here in the Library of Congress."

Jeff then got down on his knee. "Will you marry me, Lindsay Michelle Thomas?"

Lindsay saw the croaking toad of Western High changed into a handsome prince with his shining blue eyes that reflected the love stirring within him. "Of course, Jeff Ryan Wheeler."

Jewel, Troy, and the rest of the class began to clap and cheer, ignoring the visitors who passed by, staring curiously at the intimate ceremony taking place. Even a guard patrolling the area smiled at the scene.

"But," Lindsay continued, "if you think for one moment I'll agree to a wedding ceremony inside the Lincoln Memorial, you've got another guess coming."

Laughter surrounded them until Jeff stepped forward, gathered her in his arms and gave her a lengthy kiss. " 'I must have done something good. . . .' " He whispered the song from the love scene in Sound of Music.

"Something very good."

A Letter To Our Readers

Dear Reader:

In order that we might better contribute to your reading enjoyment, we would appreciate your taking a few minutes to respond to the following questions. We welcome your comments and read each form and letter we receive. When completed, please return to the following:

Fiction Editor
Heartsong Presents
PO Box 719
Uhrichsville, Ohio 44683

1. Did you enjoy reading *A Storybook Finish* by Lauralee Bliss?
   ❏ Very much! I would like to see more books by this author!
   ❏ Moderately. I would have enjoyed it more if

   _____

   _____

   _____

2. Are you a member of **Heartsong Presents**? ❏ Yes ❏ No
   If no, where did you purchase this book? _____

   _____

3. How would you rate, on a scale from 1 (poor) to 5 (superior), the cover design? _____

4. On a scale from 1 (poor) to 10 (superior), please rate the following elements.

   ____ Heroine   ____ Plot
   ____ Hero   ____ Inspirational theme
   ____ Setting   ____ Secondary characters

5. These characters were special because?_____
_____
_____

6. How has this book inspired your life?_____
_____
_____

7. What settings would you like to see covered in future **Heartsong Presents** books? _____
_____
_____

8. What are some inspirational themes you would like to see treated in future books? _____
_____
_____

9. Would you be interested in reading other **Heartsong Presents** titles? ❏ Yes ❏ No

10. Please check your age range:
   ❏ Under 18   ❏ 18-24
   ❏ 25-34   ❏ 35-45
   ❏ 46-55   ❏ Over 55

Name _____
Occupation _____
Address _____
City_____ State_____ Zip_____

Broken Things

*F*avorite **Heartsong Presents** author Andrea Boeshaar takes us into the world of a woman who courageously faces the failure of her past when she finds a faded photograph of the Chicago cop she once loved. . .but left.

Fiction • 352 pages • 5 ³/₁₆" x 8"

Please send me _____ copies of *Broken Things*. I am enclosing $11.99 for each.
(Please add $2.00 to cover postage and handling per order. OH add 6% tax.)

Send check or money order, no cash or C.O.D.s please.

Name _____

Address _____

City, State, Zip _____

To place a credit card order, call 1-800-847-8270.
Send to: Heartsong Presents Reader Service, PO Box 721, Uhrichsville, OH 44683

❤ ❤ ❤ ❤ ❤ ❤ ❤ ❤ ❤ ❤ ❤ ❤ ❤ ❤ ❤ ❤ ❤

Heart♥ong

CONTEMPORARY ROMANCE IS CHEAPER BY THE DOZEN!

Any 12 Heartsong Presents titles for only $30.00*

Buy any assortment of twelve *Heartsong Presents* titles and save 25% off of the already discounted price of $3.25 each!

*plus $2.00 shipping and handling per order and sales tax where applicable.

HEARTSONG PRESENTS TITLES AVAILABLE NOW:

___HP177 *Nepali Noon*, S. HaydenF
___HP178 *Eagles for Anna*, C. Runyon
___HP181 *Retreat to Love*, N. Rue
___HP182 *A Wing and a Prayer*, T. Peterson
___HP186 *Wings Like Eagles*, T. Peterson
___HP189 *A Kindled Spark*, C. Reece
___HP193 *Compassionate Love*, A. Bell
___HP194 *Wait for the Morning*, K. Baez
___HP197 *Eagle Pilot*, J. Stengl
___HP205 *A Question of Balance*, V. B. Jones
___HP206 *Politically Correct*, K. Cornelius
___HP210 *The Fruit of Her Hands*, J. Orcutt
___HP213 *Picture of Love*, T. H. Murray
___HP217 *Odyssey of Love*, M. Panagiotopoulos
___HP218 *Hawaiian Heartbeat*, Y.Lehman
___HP221 *Thief of My Heart*, C. Bach
___HP222 *Finally, Love*, J. Stengl
___HP225 *A Rose Is a Rose*, R. R. Jones
___HP226 *Wings of the Dawn*, T. Peterson
___HP234 *Glowing Embers*, C. L. Reece
___HP242 *Far Above Rubies*, B. Melby & C. Wienke
___HP245 *Crossroads*, T. and J. Peterson
___HP246 *Brianna's Pardon*, G. Clover
___HP261 *Race of Love*, M. Panagiotopoulos
___HP262 *Heaven's Child*, G. Fields
___HP265 *Hearth of Fire*, C. L. Reece
___HP278 *Elizabeth's Choice*, L. Lyle
___HP298 *A Sense of Belonging*, T. Fowler
___HP302 *Seasons*, G. G. Martin
___HP305 *Call of the Mountain*, Y. Lehman
___HP306 *Piano Lessons*, G. Sattler
___HP317 *Love Remembered*, A. Bell
___HP318 *Born for This Love*, B. Bancroft

___HP321 *Fortress of Love*, M. Panagiotopoulos
___HP322 *Country Charm*, D. Mills
___HP325 *Gone Camping*, G. Sattler
___HP326 *A Tender Melody*, B. L. Etchison
___HP329 *Meet My Sister, Tess*, K. Billerbeck
___HP330 *Dreaming of Castles*, G. G. Martin
___HP337 *Ozark Sunrise*, H. Alexander
___HP338 *Somewhere a Rainbow*, Y. Lehman
___HP341 *It Only Takes a Spark*, P. K. Tracy
___HP342 *The Haven of Rest*, A. Boeshaar
___HP349 *Wild Tiger Wind*, G. Buck
___HP350 *Race for the Roses*, L. Snelling
___HP353 *Ice Castle*, J. Livingston
___HP354 *Finding Courtney*, B. L. Etchison
___HP361 *The Name Game*, M. G. Chapman
___HP377 *Come Home to My Heart*, J. A. Grote
___HP378 *The Landlord Takes a Bride*, K. Billerbeck
___HP390 *Love Abounds*, A. Bell
___HP394 *Equestrian Charm*, D. Mills
___HP401 *Castle in the Clouds*, A. Boeshaar
___HP402 *Secret Ballot*, Y. Lehman
___HP405 *The Wife Degree*, A. Ford
___HP406 *Almost Twins*, G. Sattler
___HP409 *A Living Soul*, H. Alexander
___HP410 *The Color of Love*, D. Mills
___HP413 *Remnant of Victory*, J. Odell
___HP414 *The Sea Beckons*, B. L. Etchison
___HP417 *From Russia with Love*, C. Coble
___HP418 *Yesteryear*, G. Brandt
___HP421 *Looking for a Miracle*, W. E. Brunstetter
___HP422 *Condo Mania*, M. G. Chapman
___HP425 *Mustering Courage*, L. A. Coleman
___HP426 *To the Extreme*, T. Davis

(If ordering from this page, please remember to include it with the order form.)

Presents

___HP429 Love Ahoy, C. Coble
___HP430 Good Things Come, J. A. Ryan
___HP433 A Few Flowers, G. Sattler
___HP434 Family Circle, J. L. Barton
___HP438 Out in the Real World, K. Paul
___HP441 Cassidy's Charm, D. Mills
___HP442 Vision of Hope, M. H. Flinkman
___HP445 McMillian's Matchmakers, G. Sattler
___HP449 An Ostrich a Day, N. J. Farrier
___HP450 Love in Pursuit, D. Mills
___HP454 Grace in Action, K. Billerbeck
___HP458 The Candy Cane Calaboose,
        J. Spaeth
___HP461 Pride and Pumpernickel, A. Ford
___HP462 Secrets Within, G. G. Martin
___HP465 Talking for Two, W. E. Brunstetter
___HP466 Risa's Rainbow, A. Boeshaar
___HP469 Beacon of Truth, P. Griffin
___HP470 Carolina Pride, T. Fowler
___HP473 The Wedding's On, G. Sattler
___HP474 You Can't Buy Love, K. Y'Barbo
___HP477 Extreme Grace, T. Davis
___HP478 Plain and Fancy, W. E. Brunstetter
___HP481 Unexpected Delivery, C. M. Hake
___HP482 Hand Quilted with Love, J. Livingston
___HP485 Ring of Hope, B. L. Etchison

___HP486 The Hope Chest, W. E. Brunstetter
___HP489 Over Her Head, G. G. Martin
___HP490 A Class of Her Own, J. Thompson
___HP493 Her Home or Her Heart, K. Elaine
___HP494 Mended Wheels, A. Bell & J. Sagal
___HP497 Flames of Deceit, R. Dow &
        A. Snaden
___HP498 Charade, P. Humphrey
___HP501 The Thrill of the Hunt, T. H. Murray
___HP502 Whole in One, A. Ford
___HP505 Happily Ever After,
        M. Panagiotopoulos
___HP506 Cords of Love, L. A. Coleman
___HP509 His Christmas Angel, G. Sattler
___HP510 Past the Ps Please, Y. Lehman
___HP513 Licorice Kisses, D. Mills
___HP514 Roger's Return, M. Davis
___HP517 The Neighborly Thing to Do,
        W. E. Brunstetter
___HP518 For a Father's Love, J. A. Grote
___HP521 Be My Valentine, J. Livingston
___HP522 Angel's Roost, J. Spaeth
___HP525 Game of Pretend, J. Odell
___HP526 In Search of Love, C. Lynxwiler
___HP529 Major League Dad, K. Y'Barbo
___HP530 Joe's Diner, G. Sattler

Great Inspirational Romance at a Great Price!

Heartsong Presents books are inspirational romances in contemporary and historical settings, designed to give you an enjoyable, spirit-lifting reading experience. You can choose wonderfully written titles from some of today's best authors like Hannah Alexander, Andrea Boeshaar, Yvonne Lehman, Tracie Peterson, and many others.

When ordering quantities less than twelve, above titles are $3.25 each.
Not all titles may be available at time of order.

SEND TO: **Heartsong Presents** Reader's Service
         P.O. Box 721, Uhrichsville, Ohio 44683

Please send me the items checked above. I am enclosing $ _____
(please add $2.00 to cover postage per order. OH add 6.25% tax. NJ
add 6%.). Send check or money order, no cash or C.O.D.s, please.

To place a credit card order, call 1-800-847-8270.

NAME _____

ADDRESS _____

CITY/STATE _____ ZIP_____

HPS 6-03

HEARTSONG ♥ PRESENTS
Love Stories Are Rated G!

That's for godly, gratifying, and of course, great! If you love a thrilling love story but don't appreciate the sordidness of some popular paperback romances, **Heartsong Presents** is for you. In fact, **Heartsong Presents** is the only inspirational romance book club featuring love stories where Christian faith is the primary ingredient in a marriage relationship.

Sign up today to receive your first set of four, never-before-published Christian romances. Send no money now; you will receive a bill with the first shipment. You may cancel at any time without obligation, and if you aren't completely satisfied with any selection, you may return the books for an immediate refund!

Imagine. . .four new romances every four weeks—two historical, two contemporary—with men and women like you who long to meet the one God has chosen as the love of their lives. . .all for the low price of $10.99 postpaid.

To join, simply complete the coupon below and mail to the address provided. **Heartsong Presents** romances are rated G for another reason: They'll arrive Godspeed!

YES! Sign me up for Hearts ♥ng!

NEW MEMBERSHIPS WILL BE SHIPPED IMMEDIATELY!
Send no money now. We'll bill you only $10.99 postpaid with your first shipment of four books. Or for faster action, call toll free 1-800-847-8270.

NAME _____

ADDRESS _____

CITY _____ STATE _____ ZIP _____

MAIL TO: HEARTSONG PRESENTS, P.O. Box 721, Uhrichsville, Ohio 44683
or visit www.heartsongpresents.com